Through the Killing Glass

Alice in Deadland
Book II

Mainak Dhar

DEDICATION

As always, for Puja & Aaditya

ONE

WHAT ALICE REGRETTED the most about not being fully human was the fact that she could no longer cry. More than a year had passed since Alice set in motion events that had changed her life and that of everyone in the Deadland by following a Biter with bunny ears down a hole in the ground. Events that had led to the creation of a new settlement, a settlement unlike any the world had seen since The Rising. What had followed had been the re-settlement of the city of Delhi by thousands of humans who had streamed in from the Deadland to live together in a community. A community that had laws, security and houses for people to live in. A community where every night was not spent in dread of marauding Biters or raids by the Red Guards. A community that was now known simply as Wonderland.

The cost of this victory had been high. Thousands had perished in the Deadland during the struggle against the Red Guards, and hundreds more in the air raids that had been unleashed when Alice had been captured. Alice's personal costs had been high, too. She had lost her entire family, and her identity. No longer was she the mercurial fifteen year-old girl her father had doted upon. She was now the Queen of

Wonderland, whom people looked at with awe and fear. But being part-Biter, she could never taste food again; she now simply had no need for it. She could never dream of her family again, for Biters could not dream, and while she often thought back to all she had lost, she could not cry to lessen that pain, for Biters shed no tears.

To her enemies, Alice was a formidable adversary, with the training and battle-tested instincts of the most elite human soldier, but also with the inexhaustible stamina and immunity to all forms of damage short of a direct head shot that her Biter half gave her. To her human followers, she was a messiah who had rescued them from the Deadland to give them hope that they could live again like civilized people. To the Biters who followed her, she was the leader of the pack, to be followed with animal instinct and devotion.

But to herself, she was still Alice Gladwell, daughter and sister to her murdered family. She had taken her vengeance against the Red Guards, and what had begun as a mission of personal vendetta had led to something much bigger. Alice had never fashioned herself as a leader, but now she knew more than ten thousand humans in Wonderland depended on her. Whether or not she wanted this burden of leadership, it was now hers, and she was determined not to let down those who counted on her.

Much of her own young life had been spent forged in battle, and her education had consisted of little more than learning to fight and to survive in the Deadland, but today Alice was going to do something she had never done before. She was going to inaugurate the first school in Wonderland.

There was a hush among the gathered thousands as she stepped onto the makeshift podium. Arjun, her confidante and trusted advisor, had chosen the location with his usual sense of humor. The school was to be located in what had once been the Delhi Zoo.

'People of Wonderland, thank you for coming. I myself had little education beyond learning to survive in the Deadland, but now our children will learn what people did before The Rising, and one day they will revive our world the way it was.'

There was thunderous applause, but when Alice stepped off the podium, she felt a bit hollow inside. She knew nothing of what life had been like before The Rising, and while she was proud of what they had achieved together, she wondered if she was really needed in Wonderland anymore. She knew nothing of managing a city, with its squabbles over water and romantic affairs. She itched for the camaraderie she had known in the settlement where everyone knew each other, not the anonymity of urban life, where people huddled in their apartments in the center of what had once been posh government colonies in Delhi.

She saw a young couple holding hands, and she looked away. That was another experience she was never to have. She was young enough and human enough to regret never being able to be loved, but she was Biter enough to never feel such emotions. Besides, her appearance did enough to seal that deal.

As she walked back to her room in what had once been the Red Fort in the heart of Delhi, Arjun caught up with her.

'Alice, we've sent out patrols north of Wonderland again this week, but people are beginning to complain about the patrols. They say that we haven't seen Red Guards for months.'

Alice turned towards Arjun and she noted with dismay how even he flinched at her sight. Her impish smile and twinkling eyes were long gone, replaced by a vacant, yellowed gaze and skin that seemed to be rotting, giving off a foul stench. She turned away, trying not to see the expression on his face.

'Arjun, people grow fat and happy. They forget that

this safety was won with blood, and that the war still rages outside of their apartments, and any day it may visit us again.'

Arjun was with Alice—she knew that—but she also knew the pressure he faced. It was no longer popular to talk about the war. After their crippling losses in battle, the Red Guards had effectively ceded control of what had been the Deadland in North India. Occasionally a jet would be spotted high in the skies, but even they did not come lower, knowing that Wonderland's defenses bristled with hand held Surface to Air missiles wielded by experienced troopers who had once served Zeus, the mercenary arm that had done the Central Committee's bidding before they had mutinied and the Red Guards had been called in from the mainland in China.

At times like this, Alice got on her bicycle and rode alone, crossing the dried up Yamuna river to the forested area that had now been reserved for Biters. Someone had said it was like an animal reserve from before The Rising, and strangely Alice had felt herself bristle at that comment. The Biters were kept confined in a wooded area ringed by electrified fences with tunnels that allowed them to go out to the Deadland. Was the Biter part of her so strong now that she identified herself more with them than with humans? She drove with the wind blowing her flowing blond hair behind her. That was the one part of her body that had not changed when she had been transformed into the hybrid she had become.

By now, the sun was setting and darkness settling over the forests, and she saw a couple of familiar shapes. Closest to her was a Biter wearing bunny ears, with a shuffling gait and a left hand that been taken off below the elbow by a Red Guard grenade. The second was a hulking Biter wearing a hat. If Alice was the leader of the pack, then Bunny Ears and Hatter were her enforcers. After being transformed, she realized that while the Biters could not really communicate in any human language, they did communicate like animals, and had a strong pack mentality. Bringing an end to the war in the Deadland meant not just fighting the Red Guards to a bloody standstill but also ensuring that Biters and humans could at least co-exist, if not actively work together. Doing that had meant establishing herself as the leader of the pack. Now she commanded an army of thousands of Biters who emerged from the dark forest, kneeling before her.

Alice held an old, charred book in her left hand. It was the last book left in the Deadland and she had first encountered it in the underground base of the Biters in the possession of the Biter Queen. Its title was Alice in Wonderland. The Queen had believed that the book held a prophecy for healing the world, and that Alice was destined to carry out the prophecy it contained. Now that Alice had brushed up on her reading skills, she understood the coincidences leading to the Queen's belief in the 'prophecy' and Alice's part in it. Alice did not know if there was any truth to the supposed prophecy, but she did know two things. One, until someone actually sat down and wrote another book, this was indeed perhaps the last book in the Deadland, and that in itself made it a precious thing to protect, and second, that the Biters held it in an almost religious awe. That was the reason why she carried it with her every time she came to them.

Alice had come to realize that loyalty from Biters was never a given, since they were as impulsive and as aggressive as rabid animals, and when one or two of the newcomers shuffled towards her, Hatter stepped in front of them and swatted them away. Before, Alice had been disgusted by their fetid smell of rot. Now it barely bothered her.

She sat down by a tree, looking at the night sky.

But now more than stars illuminated what had once been the Deadland: lights from several apartments flickered in the dark.

'They grow complacent. They light up the settlement to be the easiest target for miles.'

She had just whispered to herself but Bunny Ears came and sat down next to her, awaiting her orders. While the Biters communicated in grunts and screeches, they seemed to understand human language to some extent. Perhaps some part of their brains still functioned despite the virus that had reduced them to this condition.

'Don't worry, Bunny Ears. Nothing I can't handle.'

She waved him away when the tactical radio strapped to her side came to life.

'White Queen, this is White Rook. Please come to the Looking Glass immediately.'

Alice got up and sped away towards the nearby temple that served as their communication center, their only real window to what was happening in the outside world. Satish—or White Rook—had named this place Looking Glass. Before he defected, Satish had been a Zeus warrior, and over time he had effectively become the head of the armed forces of Wonderland.

For months they had tried to get in touch with the ongoing resistance in what had been the United States, but without much success. Other than that, they used captured computers and handheld tablets to monitor what the Central Committee and its minions were up to. There was no news other than what the Central Committee allowed to be transmitted, but at least it gave them some idea of what was happening outside their settlement. Looking Glass had been initially located in the heart of the city, but then people had asked for it to be moved to the outskirts, since they did not really want to hear the bad news from the outside world. That was another sign that people had grown complacent, and forgotten the struggle that had won them this peace.

Alice wondered what Satish had learnt that required her to be in the Looking Glass at this time of night.

~* * * ~

'The fools want to create political parties and have an election.'

Alice could sense the disdain in Satish's voice. She knew that with relative peace, people in Wonderland had been quick to lapse into the jockeying for power that was perhaps inherent to man. It was a shame that it required something like The Rising and being hunted by Biters for men to realize that petty tokens of power and prestige were not what really mattered.

'That bastard Arun is riling everyone up, telling them we need true democracy and that they no longer need you.'

Alice tried not to get involved in the politics of men like Arun, who had been a politician before The Rising. She had continued to run Wonderland the way it had been, by a small committee of elders, and with every big decision being put to a vote.

'Satish, they will talk because they have nothing better to do. I don't think it means anything.'

Satish turned towards Alice. With all they had been through together, he saw beyond the decayed skin and yellow eyes. He still saw the incredibly brave yet naïve young girl who had done so much for everyone in the Deadland.

'Alice, you don't know how men like them work. They are no better than the leeches in the Central Committee in Shanghai. Give them half a chance and they will become tyrants in their own right.'

It was an old argument. Both Arjun and Satish hated how all they had fought for was being lost, and people were lapsing into petty politicking. A few months of security, one which they and their friends had shed blood to win, had led men like Arun to proclaim that they no longer had a war to fight, and they needed to create a more peaceful, democratic society. One where people like Alice and Satish did not need to have such a prominent role, and of course one where, conveniently enough, politicians occupied the highest rungs of the ladder.

'Satish, I'm sure you didn't call me here at this time to bitch about Arun.'

Satish slapped himself on the forehead in exaggerated apology.

'No, no, of course not. Come on, we have some exciting news. For the first time, we actually may see something of value though our Looking Glass.'

Alice followed him to a console in front of which an elderly man was sitting, hunched over a computer terminal and with headphones around his ears.

'Danish, have you got anything yet?'

Danish raised one hand as he focused on tuning the radio in front of him. Danish had been a Communications Officer in the Indian Army before The Rising, and now he was in charge of running the Looking Glass in their continuing endeavor to learn about what was happening outside Wonderland, and also to try and make contact with others like themselves.

'We've finally made contact! Check this.'

Alice peered over his shoulder to see a single message displayed on the computer screen.

'We are your brothers in arms, fighting for the independence of the United States of America. We have heard much of you and your Queen. Listen for us in a day's time.'

Danish was visibly excited, his old, wrinkled eyes twinkling as he spoke.

'They managed to get an old server up and put up this page. This is the first Internet posting in sixteen years, and looks like the Central Committee hasn't seen it yet.'

Alice had been born after The Rising, when people were more bothered about escaping from hordes of Biters than surfing the Internet, but she had seen how powerful information could be in their own struggle against the Central Committee. With tablets brought over by defecting Zeus officers, they had managed to hack into the Central Committee's Intranet. Since then they had been posting messages that led to further defections among Zeus and also started creating discontent among the masses in mainland China, who had begun to question the true nature of the war they had been sold.

Before Alice could say anything, Danish hushed her, putting on his headphones, and then passed them on to her.

'Alice, they want to talk to you.'

Alice put on the headphones and heard the crackle of static. Then there was the deep voice of a man.

'Alice, this is General Konrath of the Free American Army based out of Forth Worth, Texas. We have been fighting our own war against the same enemy you face, and we are all proud to call you a fellow American.'

Alice's father had been with the American Embassy in New Delhi before The Rising, but she had been born in a world where the countries of the old world were little more than memories. Still, it was good to make contact with people from outside the Deadland where she had been born. It made their struggle feel less lonely.

'General, we have had a few months of relative quiet in Wonderland, and the Red Guards don't really come here anymore. How are things in the United States?'

There came a pause before the general's reply.

'Alice, we are facing brutal house to house fighting against the Red Guards and the still loyal Zeus mercenaries. Our bigger problem is that we're fighting them and also fighting against the damned Biters.'

Another pause, before he added, 'You know what I mean, Alice.'

'General, there's no need to apologize. I lived in fear of Biters for the first fifteen years of my life as well.'

'Alice, I wish we had someone like you to bring peace with the Biters. But for now, we need your help. Two of our people have escaped from a labor camp of the Reds and are making their way to the plains. They have nowhere else to go, so they are trying to escape to your city. Help them if you can.'

Static muffled the connection, and then the line was terminated. Alice felt Satish exhale loudly beside her. She knew that they were being asked to re-enter a fight that many in Wonderland believed was over.

'Alice, what do you plan to do?'

Alice answered without a pause. 'Satish, I lost my entire family so we could live free. I will not allow others seeking their freedom to be hunted down when I can help them.'

Satish just sniggered.

'Satish, what are you thinking?'

Satish grinned. 'I'm thinking that fat old Arun will have a heart attack if he knows about this.'

'He doesn't have to know, does he? Well, we don't even know that they'll make it anywhere close to Wonderland.'

Danish coughed to get their attention. He had one of his tactical radios held to his ear.

'Folks, something's up. One of the advance recon parties saw a convoy of Red Guards a hundred kilometers to the north east, on the old National Highway 8. They report two trucks and some jeeps.'

'Satish, I'm getting my kit. You get some men ready and join me.'

Five minutes later, Alice was outside near her bike. Her kit consisted of a handgun in a holster strapped to her left thigh, a serrated combat knife on her right thigh, an extra handgun on an ankle holster, and an assault rifle across her back. Satish was there with three of his men, getting into their jeep.

'Alice, are you sure you want to go along? This could be a trap for all we know.'

'I'm all dressed up for the party. I cannot back out now, can I?'

As she started off on her bicycle, Satish felt a lump in his throat. The thin girl he had first met in the Deadland had become a true warrior queen, and while she looked fearsome, he still remembered the crying girl he had met in the forests of the Deadland. A girl who had just lost her family to the Red Guards. He had nearly lost her once before, to a Red Guard trap. There was no way he was going to let her down again. He checked his own assault rifle and shouted to the driver.

'What are you waiting for? Let's go!'

By the time they started, Alice was well on her way, blond hair billowing behind her. Just a couple of years ago she would have felt fear at the prospect of such imminent danger. Now she welcomed it like an old friend. Far from the petty politicking of Wonderland, now it would be the way it had been, the way she had always liked it.

~* * * ~

Alice saw that there were at least two dozen Red Guards, all wearing night vision goggles and armed with assault rifles. Their trucks were parked on the road behind them. She had left her bike a kilometer behind, tracking them the rest of the way on foot. They may have had night vision goggles and the latest equipment, but with the frontline ranks thinned by months of vicious combat, she knew from the Central Committee's Intranet that young men with no combat experience were being drafted and sent on combat missions. In contrast, she had spent her entire life training and fighting in circumstances like this. Also, one added benefit of her current state was that like Biters, she felt no fatigue. She could keep running and fighting all night long if she needed to.

Satish and his men were nearby, but for now she was alone. She saw the Red Guard officer raise his hand and shout a command in Mandarin. The Red Guards started to get back in their trucks. It seemed that they had achieved whatever they had set out to do. Alice wasn't sure what they had been up to, but she did not like it one bit. It certainly wasn't recon; they wouldn't need two large trucks and so many men for that. There was only one way to find out, and also to send a message to their masters that the Red Guards were not welcome here any more.

She raised her assault rifle to her shoulder and aimed at the officer through the night vision scope. The crosshairs were on his forehead when she shouted her warning.

'Red Guards! You are in our territory. Lay down your weapons and surrender and we will send you back unharmed.'

The Red Guards froze. Some of them muttered something she knew very well: 'Nu wu.'

'Witch' in Mandarin. Alice had come to be known among the Red Guards as the Yellow Witch, and she hoped that the fear her reputation generated would lead them to surrender. She certainly had no wish to slaughter green conscripts.

But that was not to be the case tonight. Whether driven by fear or perhaps to act brave in front of his men, the officer took out his handgun and fired in Alice's direction. That was the last mistake he made before a single round shattered his head. The Red Guards scattered, several of them firing wildly despite the fact that they were wearing night vision goggles.

Alice had her rifle on single-shot mode and was now moving in an arc around the Red Guards, picking them off one by one. Several other rifles barked and she saw three Red Guards spin and fall.

Satish and his men had joined the battle.

Sandwiched between Alice and Satish's men, the remaining Red Guards gave into wild panic and rushed towards her. Alice put her rifle down and rose to meet them, handgun in one hand and knife in the other. The first Red Guard was but feet away when she put him down with two shots. The one behind him was about to bring his rifle up to fire when Alice dove towards him, rolling on the ground and coming up in a crouch near his feet. She fired thrice, feeling more then seeing him fall as she pivoted to meet the next threat. The Red Guard she faced was terrified out of his mind and screaming incoherently, but with a rifle in his hands he was still a threat to be dealt with.

Realizing he could never get a shot off in time, he swung the rifle like a club at Alice's head. She rolled under the blow and passed the man, stabbing him twice in quick succession, getting up behind him as he fell to the ground. Another Red Guard was behind her and stabbed her with a knife in the chest. But Alice felt little more than a prick, and the man staggered back in horror as she calmly extracted the knife.

He stammered in broken English, 'Yellow Witch! Please let me go.'

Alice tossed the knife aside as she heard Satish and his men mop up the remaining resistance. The Red Guard in front of her was little more than a boy, perhaps not much older than herself. She drew closer to him and saw that he was shaking in fear.

'Go back and tell your officers that Red Guards are no longer welcome in our land.'

The man ran without hesitation and never looked back.

Satish and his men were gathering the captured

weapons and equipment. So many night vision goggles and extra ammunition were always welcome but Alice had her eyes on something else.

'Satish, those trucks would make for nice school buses.'

He smiled and then stopped on seeing the wound in Alice's chest. She caught his gaze. The wound was a couple of inches wide and there was some blood on its edges. Alice shrugged.

'It looks far worse than it feels. I'm more worried about ruining a perfectly good shirt.'

Satish grinned and continued as Alice went back to gather her rifle. Short of a direct shot to the head, Alice could not die, and she had taken more than her share of gunshots and knife wounds in the months of fierce fighting that had followed her transformation. As a result her body was crisscrossed with bloody wounds. While ordinary Biters were oblivious to these and walked about with their wounds plainly visible, Alice still retained enough of her old self to not want to be seen as she really was. So she insisted on wearing black turtleneck sweatshirts, jeans, gloves and boots at all times. It had become a trademark of hers, but nobody really knew the solitary pain behind the look.

They drove back as the sun rose over the horizon, and after changing her bloody clothes Alice went to the Council meeting that had been called that morning. She hoped that her present of two new school buses would help mollify Arun and his friends.

The dozen council members were already present when Alice arrived, including Arjun and Satish. Arun was in a corner, mumbling something to two of his friends, and when she entered the room, he rose to address her.

'Good of you join us, our Queen.'

Alice saw murder in Arjun's eyes and she gently tapped him on the shoulder as she passed him. She had no idea why Arun was so riled up this morning, but the last thing she wanted to do was to take the bait and say anything she might regret. She sat down and the meeting began.

As Wonderland had begun to take shape, Alice had gained a new appreciation for all the complexities her father had to deal with as one of the leaders of their settlement in the Deadland. Fights over food supplies, disputes over who took how much of the communal pool of clean drinking water, cases of adultery and of people getting into fights after having too much to drink—all the problems that ironically came with humans becoming more civilized and living in more settled communities. Today was no different, and they talked about the banalities of running the community for some time. Alice noticed that Arun seemed on edge, as if he was dying to say something. Alice tried to work out what it could be—and then, when the discussion turned to security, she realized what it was.

As the head of security within Wonderland, Arjun first rose to give his update. 'Folks, no real crime to report since last week, unless you count the Chopra kid getting drunk and taking a leak in front of Arun's house as an offense.'

Everyone laughed, and Alice was once again grateful as to how the salesman turned guerilla leader turned security chief seemed to have a natural talent for defusing tension. But things took a turn for the worst when Satish rose to give his update on external security.

'Thankfully, not much excitement to report outside either. The Red Guards have been relatively quiet in our neighborhood. Intranet reports show that the Central Committee is dealing with enough unrest in China and a very tough war in America to pay us much attention. We do have some big news to report, though.'

Everyone seemed to sit up as he continued, 'We made contact with the Americans last night.'

There was a palpable buzz in the room as Satish outlined what had been said, but before he could talk about the incident involving the Red Guards, Arun stood up.

'Alice, the Red Guards no longer bother us and we enjoy a peace we have not known for years. Why did you then provoke war with your ambush last night?'

Alice was not entirely surprised. Many of Satish's men had taken up wives in the settlement and word would have spread.

'We did not ambush anyone. There was a large force of Red Guards well within our territory, and we gave them a chance to surrender. When they fired, we had to defend ourselves.'

Arun glared at her, his jowls almost shaking as he contained his anger. He had been a politician before The Rising, and Alice knew that in Wonderland, he finally saw his chance at gaining that kind of power again. The problem was that she came in his way. He knew that many people in Wonderland would unquestioningly follow the young girl who had brought them together and lost so much on their behalf rather than trust him—once a career politician, and a man who had joined them only after the worst of the fighting was over.

Alice adopted a more conciliatory tone. 'Arun, we got two buses I thought the school could use. Moreover, whatever the Red Guards were up to, they would have got the message that they cannot come here anymore.'

The subject dropped, but Arun moved onto something else to needle Alice.

'What news of those Biters?'

Alice's eyes narrowed at the contempt in his tone.

'They are well within the area we had decided to give to them, and I have people in charge who I can trust.'

'People indeed.'

Several other sniggers whispered through the room.

Alice's voice took on a new edge. 'You all seem to have forgotten that we would never have defeated the Red Guards without the thousands of Biters who died acting as our foot soldiers.'

'They owe us no loyalty or love, Alice. They are animals that follow only you. I want our children to grow up without their shadow, to grow up like civilized people did before The Rising.'

Satish stepped in on Alice's behalf. 'Arun, the Biters cause us no problems now. Just let it be and let's move on.'

Just then, the door swung open and two people walked in. Alice recognized them as two of Arjun's men who had been assigned to do the rounds of Wonderland during the daytime. They both looked ashen-faced and their hands and clothes were covered with blood.

Alice had left her other weapons in her room, but still had her handgun. Instinctively she gripped it, ready for action.

'What happened? Did the Red Guards attack?'

One of the men looked at Alice, a snarl of hatred forming on his face.

'It was the damn Biters. They slaughtered our kids!'

TWO

A LICE RACED OUT of the building and rode her bike as fast as she could towards the area where the incident had taken place. Ten children of between eight and ten years of age had been taken for a trip by their teacher. Their first day at the new school was to have been a special treat, a visit to the old airport where they were to learn of how the city had been once, how the Red Guards had used the airport to fly out settlers from the Deadland to work in labor camps, and also learn about the famous battles waged there against the Red Guards.

As Alice dismounted, she saw the pick-up truck that had carried them there on the side of the road. She could not see any bodies yet, but the stench of death was unmistakable in the air. Some people had already arrived, most of them parents of the kids who had gone on the trip. One of the mothers, a recent entrant to Wonderland whom Alice did not know well, lunged at her.

'You monster! See what your people have done.'

Her husband held her back as she continued screaming.

Laying eyes on the bodies, Alice cursed that she could not cry. Biters did not shed tears, but her heart broke and she fell to her knees as she saw the torn bodies strewn across the field beside the road. The teacher, a young man called Gaurav, had tried to protect the children, and from the looks of it had gone down fighting. His right hand still gripped the pistol he carried—but that was about the only intact part of his body. The rest of him had been torn to ribbons. Even with the relative peace they enjoyed, no adult went about unarmed, yet nobody had thought that an innocent school trip would have required more protection or heavier firepower.

Satish and Arjun caught up and jumped out of their jeep to run to the scene of the carnage. Both had seen brutal combat up close, but the slaughter of innocent children was too much even for them. Arjun had tears streaming down his face and he put his hand on Alice's shoulder.

'Alice, we need to get you out of here now.'

Alice looked up. 'I have to be here. These are my people. These are the same people I promised I would keep safe. These...'

Her words dwindled to silence as Arun had come up to join them. He knelt and retched at the sight before him. He looked at Alice, his face pale.

'What have your Biters done? What have you brought upon us?'

Alice was too stunned to reply. She had sacrificed everything: her family, and ultimately her humanity, so that the people who depended on her could live in safety. So that she could fulfill her father's last wish that she not let her people down and lead them to a better life. She lived a tortured existence where she could feel some human emotions but never act on them. And now, in one fell swoop, the same people she had done nothing but help, asking for nothing in return, were casting her off.

She felt strong arms grip her and Arjun guided her away. She noticed that Satish had his assault rifle in his hands. She was about to ask him if that was necessary when she saw several of the men around Arun with their guns drawn. Arjun bundled her into his jeep and Satish joined them as they drove off. Alice just sat there, her shaking hands the only sign of the turmoil she felt inside. What had just happened?

When she asked Satish where they were going, he replied grimly, 'The Looking Glass. If there's trouble, we can at least defend ourselves there.'

The drive was taken in silence. When they arrived, they saw Danish standing at the entrance, a shotgun in hand. It was the first time Alice had seen him with a gun.

The Looking Glass was in a temple complex, with the main communications room in what had once been the glass-fronted office. When he had set it up, Satish had been clear it needed to be defensible against Red Guard assaults, so there were two hardened positions on the roof from where his men could fire man-portable ground to air missiles. Those would be of no use today, but there was one remotely controlled gun turret that they had captured from a Red Guard base. That had been installed on an elevated position on the roof, offering 360-degree coverage. As Alice entered the Looking Glass, she shuddered at what things had come to. She would never have imagined using these defenses against her own people, and hoped it never came to that.

Inside, Alice sat in silence, trying to understand what she had seen. Arjun looked at her and shook his head sadly. Danish was sitting quietly in a corner. Gaurav had been a good friend of his, and he looked devastated.

'Arjun, it could not have been one of the Biters around Wonderland!'

'Alice, Biters did kill those kids. No man could have torn them apart like that. While it's possible that a band of outside Biters crept in, there's no way we can prove anything.'

Danish spoke up, having got a message from one of his men in the city. 'There's a mob headed our way. This could get ugly.'

'Alice, there are people who love you and would die for you, but with so many deaths, people are losing their minds. Let Arjun and me try and cool things down. The Looking Glass is set up to be defended, so if it comes to a fight, we can make a stand here.'

'Make a stand? Mobs? God, Satish, listen to yourself. This is our own Wonderland, our home.'

Arjun spoke up for the first time. 'Satish is right. Human mobs are every bit as dangerous as a Biter horde. They won't think; they won't ask questions. We need to get some sense into people's heads before anyone gets to you.'

Taking Danish into a corner, Arjun said, 'You can go if you want. You don't have to stay.'

Danish sat down at his console. 'I lost my family in The Rising, and then lived like a rat for years. The only purpose I have in my life now is helping us stay in touch with the world through the Looking Glass, and the only family I have is the people of Wonderland. Both of those I owe to Alice. I will not desert her now. You thugs do what you need to do; I need to keep the Looking Glass running.'

Satish used the radio to get in touch with his teams. Most of his men were part of his original unit at Zeus and had fought side by side with Alice since they first met up. They were fiercely loyal to her and he knew they would fight for her if it came to it.

'White Rook One, this is White Rook. Get to the Looking Glass to reinforce positions.'

Alice touched his arm, shaking her head.

'No, Satish. I will not have our people turn on each other because of me. Tell your men to stay away and not get involved in the fight.'

Alice looked at the feed from the camera mounted on top of the Looking Glass. A mob of at least a hundred men was approaching, among their numbers some of the fathers to the dead children. All of them were armed, and one or two carried half-full bottles of alcohol. Arun was with them, and while he was not egging them on, he was not doing anything to try and stop them either.

'He wants to be a leader, and is now no more than a common rabble-rouser. He should be the one talking some sense into the younger ones. Instead, he leads them.'

Without even waiting for Alice to suggest it, Satish had moved the joystick controlling the gun turret, swiveling it until it was aimed at the approaching mob.

'They won't last more than ten seconds if I let go on full auto.'

The mob stopped, knowing they would be seriously outmatched if it came to a fight. The only way for someone to take the Looking Glass was with heavy anti-tank weapons or RPGs, and the only ones with such weapons in Wonderland were Satish's forward recon teams.

Alice touched Satish's arm and she felt him flinch at the contact, once more aware of how different she was now. Her touch had none of the warmth it once held. It was now as cold as a corpse.

'No, Satish. There will be no more killing here today.'

'Bring the Biter bitch out!'

Satish stepped out, his rifle at his shoulder.

'Which son of a whore said that? Step forward if you're man enough to back those words up!'

No answer came. Satish turned furiously to Arun.

'These men look up to you. Ask them to go back home. We can all talk when people cool down.'

'Cool down? My son was torn apart by her kind, and you ask me to cool down? We should have destroyed the Biters, but we had to tolerate their presence because of her.'

Satish turned on the man who had just spoken and looked him in the eye.

'Jai, you do remember that I took a bullet to save your family when the Red Guards came? I also share your grief and want to punish those responsible, but don't turn on Alice or rush to conclusions.'

Arjun was now outside, with Alice beside him. The big man strode forward, and while he had his gun holstered, Alice saw several of the men lower their guns as he approached. Satish had been an invaluable soldier in their struggle, but he was a relative newcomer. In contrast, Arjun had been leading his band of 'Ruin Rats' for years, helping them survive against Biters and Zeus troopers alike. Many of the men in the crowd had been part of his original crew, and looked away as he addressed them.

'Jai, Ritesh, Ankush...all of you were my brothers. Brothers who bled and fought with me.'

Alice saw some of the men sheepishly put away their weapons as Arjun continued.

'But today you insult that bond by turning on a girl who has perhaps sacrificed more than all of us. Give her a chance, that's all I ask of you.'

Alice now stepped forward. She had left all her weapons inside the Looking Glass.

'I did not choose to be this way. I too want to play with my sister and eat meals with my parents. I too want to go to school and learn something other than killing people. But I have no regrets, for in all that loss we had created a bigger family than I ever had. A family called Wonderland. I promise to personally bring to justice those who have done this to your families and children, but please trust me at least this much. For all we've been through together, please give me this much trust, and let me find out who was behind this. If it was one of the Biters in Wonderland, I promise you I will spare none of them.'

Whether it was the impact of her words, Arjun's

cajoling, or the simple fact that through the entire exchange the gun turret had been trained on the group, they grudgingly dispersed, leaving only Arun. He walked up to Alice and she half expected him to say something sarcastic or provocative. Instead, he looked genuinely shell-shocked.

'Alice, I know we've had our differences. I know that in the last few months people have been questioning why we still live in a state of war when there is no war to be fought, and I know that yet others question why we keep the Biters close at hand. But I'm willing to forget all of that if you help us find out who was responsible for this massacre.'

Alice looked at him, trying to gauge whether he was sincere or he just wanted to maintain the status quo since that best served his political agenda. She was perhaps too young to judge and took him at face value.

'Arun, we have known some measure of peace, but the world outside is still at war. I know we situated Looking Glass outside the center of Wonderland because you thought people would get alarmed at all the bad news. The reality is we cannot pretend away the fact that the world is still bleeding, and today some of that blood seeped into Wonderland.'

Arun looked away sheepishly as Arjun took up where Alice had left off.

'Arun, you and others had voted to reduce patrols and cancel regular combat training. We cannot pretend this is the Delhi the way it was before the Rising. We know peace now, but that might change at any moment. Let us get to the bottom of today's killing, but you as an elder need to help people understand that things are much more dangerous outside Wonderland than they may want to believe.'

Suitably chastised, Arun went back, and then Alice mounted her bike.

'Alice, do you want me to come?'

Alice refused Satish's offer. This was something she

25

had to do alone. Maintaining her composure had been necessary in front of the bereaved families, but now she was gripped with fury. Whoever had killed those children would pay dearly.

~* * * ~

The groaning Biter went down on his back, his hand cracking in several places as Alice twisted it and threw him over her shoulder. Before he had been turned, he had been a slight old man, but there was no sympathy or pity in Alice's eyes as she kicked him, dislocating his chin. That did nothing to improve his face, which already had skin peeling off in several places and an ear missing from a gunshot.

'What lunacy made you let outsiders into Wonderland?'

She was not sure how much he understood, but she was so angry she really did not care. The Biter was now on his knees, snarling, all obedience to Alice gone. His teeth were bared, jagged and covered with dried blood. He snapped as she came closer but she easily weaved out of the way. In the time she had spent with the Biters, she knew that they would only obey a leader who spoke from a position of strength. With Dr. Protima, their first Queen, who had first opened Alice's eyes to the true nature of the Biters and the conspiracy behind The Rising, that authority had come from her ability to speak and reason like a human and her possession of the tattered copy of Alice in Wonderland that the Biters had come to revere as their holy relic. For Alice, that authority was backed up by her combat skills honed in years of fighting to survive in the Deadland.

The Biter lunged at her again, and this time Alice caught his right hand, snapping it back and then bringing the heel of her own right hand snapping against his nose. The blow would have killed a grown man, but Biters did not die so easily. The Biter fell back and struggled to get back up, his face mangled and bloody, when Alice took out her combat knife and stabbed him through the head. He did not get back up again.

Alice had come to the Biters' reserve and told Hatter and Bunny Ears about what had happened. They knew the potential implications and she sensed their panic, and within minutes they had brought the old Biter in front of her. He had screeched and groaned as if pleading for mercy, but the hand gestures Hatter made were clear enough. This Biter had let in a band of outsiders in return for a thick bunch of ganja leaves that some of the Biters favored. Pleading had soon given away to a desperate attempt to escape as the Biter, like a cornered animal, had turned on Alice. That had been his last mistake.

As the adrenaline wore off, Alice tried to calm herself down and looked at Hatter and Bunny Ears. Hatter looked imposing, standing well over six feet tall and built like a tank. The hat he guarded with such pride still stood atop his head. He had suffered more than his share of wounds over the years: at least six bullet holes were visible on his chest and bites too numerous to count crisscrossed his body. His eyes were dilated and red, and his yellowed face was covered with dried blood. Just a year ago, Alice would have run in terror at such a sight. Today he seemed to be cowering before her.

'Hatter, what the hell happened? I told you to make sure everyone stays here and does not wander.'

Bunny Ears had his head down, like a pet that had just been disciplined. His face was still contorted in what at first glance appeared to be a lopsided grin, but Alice figured out later had been the result of a gash drawn across his face by Biter nails when he had been bitten and turned.

'You do know what people will want to do, don't

you? They will start hunting you down again!'

At this, Hatter looked at her and a low growl came from the back of his throat. Alice sighed.

'Yes, and you will fight, won't you? And then we'll be back where we were. Tearing ourselves apart while the Red Guards and their masters rule over us.'

Not wanting to face any of the affected families, Alice did not go back to the city center but instead went back to the Looking Glass. Danish was there, as usual, playing with his computers and radio equipment.

'Danish, anything new?'

He tapped on the monitor in front of him. 'The Americans posted again.'

Alice leaned over and read the message.

Free American forces under Colonel Barnett swept aside Red Guards at New Orleans, and are linking with other forces to press the offensive to liberate the city. If you are anywhere near, find safety or join the fight.

'They seem to have their communications working again,' she said, 'How did they manage that?'

'America was much more developed than India, and I suspect their Armed Forces and government would have had secure and protected networks and servers. They were ready to survive a nuclear apocalypse with Russia at one time, so something must have survived. Also, in India hardly anyone other than the Police and Armed Forces had guns since public gun ownership was limited. In the US, lots of people had their own guns, so it was easier to fight back when they needed to. I think it just took time for them to regroup and get over the shock of the Biters to start organizing. Plus, I was on the radio with them earlier today. They think we helped a lot.'

'How did we help?'

'Our postings and messages first started causing dissension in Zeus. Before The Rising, Zeus was an American Private Military Contractor, so most of their senior officers were American, especially ex-military folks. When the news started coming out that the whole mess had been orchestrated by elements in China and some American elites, many of them revolted. We're much closer to China, so significant Red Guard reinforcements came faster. In America, that took more time, and by then the Zeus deserters and local settlers had made a lot of headway.'

Alice had to ask the next question given what she had been through over the day.

'Danish, what about the Biters in America?'

Danish looked away.

'Well, they hear that it's more like a disease, that they can be lived with—they hear about you. But they're not buying it. I can't blame them. Remember how things were here before you got here? They hunt down Biters and burn them. They call it a Biter Barbeque. Not pretty.'

That night was anxious for Alice, spent wondering how she could possibly keep things from exploding. The next morning, she did what she thought was the right thing to do. She went to visit each of the families who had lost children in the attack. She told them about what had happened in the Biter Reservation and promised them that she would not allow such a thing to happen again.

Then she called Arjun and Satish for a meeting in her room.

'Guys, there is no way such a thing can take place ever again. I've told Hatter and Bunny Ears, but you know that discipline is too much to expect from every Biter out there. So we need to help.'

'What do you have in mind?'

'Arjun, we need more security patrols inside Wonderland to watch the borders from the inside.'

Arjun sadly shook his head. 'It's not as simple as that now we number so many. Now we'd need it voted in the Council, and you know how Arun and his friends feel.'

'Come on, they would think differently after the attack, wouldn't they?'

Arjun looked at Alice grimly. He realized that for all her combat skills she was but a child, and unschooled in the murky world of politics that Arun had mastered.

'Alice, Arun was very nice to you when he last met you, but he's been telling anyone who'll listen that he doesn't believe the story about it being Biters from the outside. He says he's sure it was Biters from the Reservation. He won't vote to increase patrols; he'd much rather put the blame on you for being too soft on the Biters.'

Alice gritted her teeth. 'So what does he want to do?'

'He hasn't said it out loud as such, but he thinks we should move the Biters far away, and of course, he'd rather he run this place all by himself as leader instead of a Council where you have such a large say given your past. That's why he keeps asking for elections for a single leader.'

Satish broke his silence. 'I can help.'

Both Arjun and Alice looked at him as he elaborated.

'I could have two of my recon teams come in closer to the city centre.'

Arjun spotted the obvious problem in the suggestion. 'We send the deep recon boys out to watch for Red Guard incursions and wild bands of Biters to intercept them before they get close. Your move would leave us exposed.'

'Yes, but only till the situation stabilizes.'

Alice shook her head. 'Word will get out. Some of those boys will speak to their wives in the city. Others will talk too much over a drink. Arun and his friends will throw a fit and accuse us of overriding them.'

Just then, Alice's tactical radio crackled to life.

'White Queen, this is Looking Glass.'

It was Danish.

'Looking Glass, what do you have to report?'

'One of our recon teams called in and said that they found fresh footprints, many of them, leading into the city. I don't know how they evaded our patrols, but they say the footprints must be of Biters by the way they seem to have moved. Then Rahul down at the farms just called on his radio, saying he saw what seemed to be a group of Biters down the road.'

The words sent a chill down Alice's spine. Satish and Arjun had both heard the transmission and they knew what the implications of another Biter attack would be. Without a word being said between them, they gathered their weapons. Alice was the first out the door, and roared down the road on Danish's bike, with Satish and Arjun following closely behind in a jeep. There was no time to call for reinforcements. They would have to handle this themselves.

Alice remembered the bodies of the children and vowed to make these Biters pay dearly for what they had done.

~* * * ~

Alice cursed as her first burst went wide, and the Biters in front of her scattered behind the bushes overlooking the farmlands north of the city center where the Biters had been reported. Alice had let her anger get the better of her and fired even before her bike had come to a complete halt. Firing her assault rifle one-handed and on the move was something her trainers back at her settlement would have frowned upon, but then they had also always advised her never to fight angry.

Stilling her mind she slipped off the bike, selecting single-shot mode on her assault rifle. Spraying rounds was hardly a smart tactic when all that mattered was putting one round into a Biter's head.

There.

She saw a Biter round the corner and she aimed and put a round into his chest. The Biter staggered back and bared his teeth at her when another round drilled him through the head. Another Biter was coming up just behind her to the right and Alice swiveled towards him, firing at him. One shot, one kill. By now Arjun and Satish had joined the battle and were firing away. Alice saw Arjun kick a large Biter down and step on his chest before shredding the Biter's head with automatic fire. Clearly she was not the only one who was fighting angry today—but given the scene of the slaughtered children, it was no surprise.

That momentary distraction almost cost her dearly. A gnarled, bloody hand swept at her face, scratching her just below the eyes. She turned towards the Biter, looking at her with red eyes, his skin coming off in bloody patches. She brought her rifle around in an arc, shattering his jaw. Then she kicked his feet from under him and shot him twice in the head.

The shooting had stopped.

'Did we get them all?'

Satish was not about to let his guard down and swept the area, his rifle raised. Arjun kicked one of the Biters to make sure he was gone. It twitched, so he fired into the back of its head.

'I think we got all the bastards now.'

The three of them looked at each other for some time, mixed emotions coursing through all of them. They had not been in such an intense fight this far inside Wonderland for many months, and certainly they had all thought that the days of defending against Biter hordes was over. However, along with that concern came a sense of catharsis. They had avenged the deaths of the children, and while nothing would bring the kids back, this would hopefully start bridging some of the rifts that had been created between Alice and the settlers who seemed to favor Arun.

Satish and Arjun took a break, taking out their water bottles. They were about to go back to their jeep when Alice noticed something.

'Guys, something is not right here.'

They stopped and looked where she was pointing.

'Check out their faces and bodies. They are decomposed like Biters, but they don't have too many visible wounds other than the rounds we put in them. Normally they're covered with unhealing wounds from their conversion. These guys are barely scratched.'

Satish peeled off the clothes of a Biter at his feet with his knife and stepped back, shocked.

'Shit, this one has a totally clean body.'

Arjun was still taking it all in.

'Maybe they got infected recently. Maybe that's why there aren't too many wounds.'

Alice wasn't satisfied.

'Could a dozen of them be infected at the same time? All of them without a single visible bite or scratch mark?'

Just then Satish heard a message coming over his radio in the jeep. He ran to it and picked up the mike. As he spoke, Alice saw the color leave his face.

'Satish, what happened?'

He looked her, a fear in his eyes that Alice had never seen before, even in the thick of combat against the Red Guards.

'Alice, come on. We need to get you to the Looking Glass. That's the only safe place I can think of now till things cool down.'

'What happened?'

Satish looked at her, his eyes filling with tears. 'This was a decoy. Another group of Biters got into the city. They got to some apartments before some of the men stopped them. They're saying more than twenty of us are dead, most of them women and children. Some of the Biters got away, but they killed eight of them. From what Danish said, they seem to be the same sort as the ones we killed.'

Alice held onto the side of the jeep for support, trying to comprehend what was happening.

'Biters don't use tactics like these. I don't understand what is going on.'

Satish grabbed her hand and pushed her towards the jeep. 'We'll figure all that out later. Now we need to get you to safety.'

'Safety? Satish, this is my home. We started this place together. I am not going to hide in my own home.'

As soon as she finished her sentence, a bullet whizzed past her, missing her head by inches. Driven by instinct and training, Alice rolled to her right, bringing up her handgun in a two-handed grip, aiming at where the shot had come from. The shooter was a young boy, perhaps no more than twelve years old, carrying a rifle that was too heavy for him. He was crying and had blood covering his shirt.

'Your Biters killed my brother!'

Alice lowered her handgun, too shocked to react, when Arjun snatched the gun away from the boy. Satish was still on the radio and Danish spoke with renewed urgency.

'Don't bring the White Queen here. My men report that a large mob is headed here, and another group is on its way to the Biter Reservation. They're saying that it's time to wipe out the Biters.'

Satish put the radio down.

'A war with the Biters will destroy Wonderland, and everything we've created.'

THREE

'**H**ATTER, I KNOW you did not do this, but we don't have time to prove or explain anything!'

As soon as they had got the news, Alice and Satish had rushed to the Biter Reservation on Danish's bike, while Arjun had headed to the Looking Glass, both to try and pacify the people headed there and also to keep Danish safe. Danish was not as closely associated with Alice as Satish was, but neither did he have any qualms about making his distaste for Arun known publicly. Alice had gathered the Biters and told them what had happened and their reaction was clear. Even without human language, their surprise and indignation was apparent.

Hatter reared up to his full height, roaring in frustration. Alice reached out, touching the rough, bloodied skin on his hand.

'If you fight the humans today then all will be lost. We will be back to what our lives had been like in the Deadland, fighting and slaughtering each other, and then the Red Guards and their masters would have won. Do you understand what I am asking you to do?'

Hatter had put his head down, but refused to acknowledge what Alice had just asked. Bunny Ears, however, stood next to him and emitted a low keening sound. Alice knew that he was sad, much like a pet being asked to go away, but that he would listen to her. Alice just wanted them to get out of sight while she tried to figure out where the attacking Biters had come from, and also try and cool things down with people in Wonderland.

Within minutes, there was no sign of the Biters. They had disappeared down the warren of underground tunnels and bomb shelters where Alice had first encountered them. Arun and his closest supporters were relative newcomers and would have no idea of the full extent of the tunnel network. The ones who had some idea of where the tunnels opened were the recon teams that worked for Satish, and they would not betray him or Alice.

'Satish, come on! Let's get to the Looking Glass.'

As she started the bike, they got their first glimpse of the approaching mob. There were more than a hundred men on foot, some carrying lit torches, and all of them armed. As they saw Alice speed away, a couple of them fired, sending dust and gravel flying all around her as Alice rode away. The fact that they had opened fire without even giving her a chance to explain meant that things had totally gone out of control. She also knew that sending the Biters into hiding would only make her and the Biters look even guiltier, but that was a better option than the bloodbath that would have followed otherwise.

When they approached the Looking Glass, Alice knew that something was wrong. Arjun had driven in Satish's jeep, and now it was lying on the side of the road, pockmarked with bullet holes and with its windshield shattered. Anxious about her friend, Alice jumped off the bike and was about to run to the Looking Glass when Satish grabbed her hand.

'This could be an ambush. Let's not rush into it.'

Both of them unslung their assault rifles and approached the temple complex.

Alice said, 'I saw some movement near

the doorway.'

Satish knelt down, looking through his scope. 'There's someone hiding there.'

Alice crept along the far wall while Satish hid behind the jeep, covering the doorway. Alice did not want to harm any of the people of Wonderland—after all, they were like family. But if any of them had hurt Arjun, there would be hell to pay.

Alice was now just feet away from the doorway and she dove in front of it, coming up with her rifle raised. She saw Arjun sitting huddled against the door. He had his rifle in his hands, but there was a small pool of blood forming under him, and he was struggling to keep his eyes open.

'Arjun, no!'

Hearing Alice's anguished shout, Satish ran over and they took Arjun inside the complex. Danish was there, his hands and face cut. Some of the glass surrounding the communications room had been shattered and there were three bodies lying among the bloodied glass fragments. The men wore filthy, dust-covered clothes of the sort that Alice had not seen since her people formed Wonderland.

Satish was tending to Arjun's wounds while Danish filled them in on what had happened.

'They heard that you were headed to the Reservation so most of them went there. That bastard Humpy Dumpty ordered the mob to go there. I heard him myself on the radio.'

Humpty Dumpty was Danish's preferred term for Arun, in reference to his weight and nearly bald head.

'Arjun and I were here when these three bastards came to kill us. These were not our people, Alice. They are stragglers from the Deadland someone must have hired to do their dirty work. I bet some of them are mixed in with the mobs, riling them up. Arjun took them all out, but they managed to shoot him.'

Alice took it in, but her mind refused to believe it.

There were still people out in the Deadland, mostly small groups of bandits who had terrorized the settlements before Wonderland had been formed. Alice had steadfastly refused to let any of them into Wonderland. Alice knew they would have hated her for that decision, but to think that someone from inside Wonderland had let them in to kill her was too much to believe. Satish would have seen her doubt.

'Alice, you are still too young to know how messed up people can be when they want power. I don't have any trouble believing Arun could have done this. I say we get my boys and bust him.'

'No. No.'

Everyone started at Arjun's words. He struggled to sit. Satish had bandaged the wound on his thigh, but he was clearly weak from the loss of blood.

'No, Satish. That would mean civil war, and ordinary folks would believe that Alice and our Biters were guilty of the attacks and side with Arun. We would destroy Wonderland.'

'What, then?'

'Look, these three goons here are obviously Deadlander bandits and even if Arun hired them, he would never own up to it publicly. But people are baying for blood and I can't blame them. So many families have lost people in the last two days that they aren't thinking straight.'

'So what do we do, Arjun?'

'Alice, you need to find out who's behind this. Those Biters were inserted here for these attacks, and someone human, someone very smart, thought it all up. But you can't do that from the inside. You need to get back to the Deadland and find out what's going on.'

'What about you?'

'Hey, I'll just say these bandits hurt me, which is true enough, and that I've got no idea where you are. Remember, I used to sell useless vacuum cleaners for a living to people who didn't need them. I can sell Arun any story I want.'

Arjun smiled as he said the words, but there was a pained grimace apparent on his face. Alice took a look around, weighing the decision before her.

'Danish, radio the folks in town, telling them bandits attacked the Looking Glass, and ask for medical help. Tell nobody we were here.'

Danish looked at her, grim determination on his face.

'Alice, you can trust me. Here, take this so you can know what's going on inside and I can tell you what Humpty Dumpty is up to.'

Alice gratefully took the portable radio set he had given her and put it in her backpack. She was about to leave when Satish joined her.

'I'm coming with you.'

'Satish, you don't have to...'

He never let her finish. 'We've fought too many battles together for me to let you go alone on this one.'

And so Alice and Satish walked out through the shattered glass facade of the Looking Glass, the bloodied glass fragments crunching under their feet as they set out for their trip back into the Deadland.

~* * * ~

General Chen watched the black helicopter glide in and land in a far corner of the airfield. It was always cold in Ladakh, where he was based, but he felt a chill go through him that had nothing to do with the temperature. After he had surrendered a forward base to Alice and her forces, he had been stripped of his command of the Red Guard forces in the Deadland, and had been sent to an indoctrination camp near Guangzhou. The Central Committee propaganda machine called these camps 'holiday camps for tired veterans to recuperate and regain their revolutionary fervor.' In reality, it was a torture camp where veterans who had become politically inconvenient or had started asking uncomfortable questions were shipped out. Like the purges of all dictators in the past, those who were perhaps most capable of defending the regime were punished, because the best soldiers are also those who dare to think. Chen had made that mistake when he surrendered his base to Alice to prevent his men from being slaughtered. He had been an officer in the Chinese Red Army before The Rising, and with the nuclear and biological weapon exchanges with the Americans and the chaos enveloping the world in the days that followed, he had devoted himself to defending his people against the Biters. It had been a clear-cut mission, one where he had little doubt as to whether he was doing the right thing or not. That was until he learnt of this girl called Alice and the stories she was spreading. He had dismissed them as propaganda, and had captured her once, intending to send her to the mainland for execution. But something had changed when he had looked at her during her attack on the Red Guard base he had been inspecting close to a year ago. He had seen the Biters following her, had seen that she was not quite human, yet not Biter either. That had planted the seeds of doubt in his mind, and he had confided to a brother officer back in Shanghai. He had raised questions about whether what the Central Committee had been telling the people about the true nature of the Biters and the war in the Deadland was entirely true. That more than his battlefield surrender had been his undoing. Chen's only relief was that his wife had been spared the horrors of the camp.

He had been rehabilitated just six months later and re-instated with all honors, to be sent to the new base at Ladakh where the Red Guards kept a watch on the community called Wonderland. It had been nothing more than glorified sentry duty and he had begun to wonder why he had been spared. Then the stealthy black helicopter he had just seen land had arrived and started going out on sorties to the Deadland. Its crew and passengers had been flown in from Shanghai and even though he was the base commander, Chen had not been allowed any access to them. They stayed in their own quarters behind a walled complex, and did not report to him.

He wondered what the old men in the Central Committee were up to now, but knew that whatever it was, the cost in blood would be paid by the young conscripts he was now supposed to lead.

~* * * ~

The dust was swirling around her and Alice had the hood on her sweatshirt pulled up around her face. She had grown up in the Deadland, but just a few months of living in the relative comfort of Wonderland told her just how brutal and uncompromising life in the Deadland could be in comparison. When she had lived there with her family in their settlement, conventional wisdom was that no human could survive in the Deadland unless they were in a large, organized group. The Deadland was teeming with predators, Biter and human alike, and now Satish and Alice would have to contend with them on their own if they were to try and solve the mystery of the Biter attacks. Alice knew that Bunny Ears, Hatter and her other Biters would be close at hand through their network of hidden underground tunnels, but there was no way for her to contact them, and depending on them to show up when she needed help was hardly a good survival strategy.

'Alice, my boys told me that this was the only sector they did not patrol yesterday. If the attackers came into Wonderland from the outside, then it must have been through here.'

It was now getting dark, and Satish suggested that they rest. Alice was not going to get tired from walking, and Satish was a professional soldier who could keep going for some hours yet. However, they did not want to take the chance of bumping into unwelcome company in the darkness.

Alice hid the bike in the bushes and then called out, 'Up the trees.'

Satish looked at Alice incredulously.

'Come on, are you serious? Do we have to hang from branches like Tarzan?'

That puzzled Alice; she came from a time after cartoons had ceased to exist, and she had no idea who or what Tarzan was.

'No, because Biters cannot climb trees, and we'll see bandits while they're far away.'

Satish grunted at the wisdom and clambered up a tree. Taking the adjoining tree, Alice whispered, 'Take a nap. I'll keep watch.'

About two hours later, Alice heard a rustling noise nearby. She raised her rifle, looking through the night vision scope to see three men walking towards them. They were armed, though it looked like they carried a motley collection of homemade pistols and an antique looking shotgun; the hallmarks of Deadland bandits. But despite the nature of the weapons, Alice knew that men such as these could be deadly.

As the men sat down and proceeded to take some food out, Alice relaxed. They had no idea Alice and Satish were sitting just a few feet above them, and they would soon hopefully be on their way.

Then she saw something that made her take a closer look. One of the bandits was taking something out of a bag. Only it was not just any bag. It was a child's bag, cobbled together from old clothes, patched together by a loving mother, embellished with cartoon characters that the child must have heard of in tales told by the adults who had experienced them on screen and in books before The Rising. There was only one place in the Deadland where such a bag could be found now: in Wonderland. And it was likely that this had been made as a school bag for a child who had been murdered just two days ago.

Something snapped inside Alice, and she took a signal flare from her backpack and threw it to the ground, blinding the three men. Before they could gather their wits, Alice was in front of them, her rifle pointed at them.

'Where did you get that bag?'

One of the men made the fatal mistake of thinking they were faced with a mere girl, and he brought up his pistol. Alice snapped off a three round burst, hitting him in the chest and slamming him against the tree behind him. The noise had awakened Satish and he whistled to let the men below him know that he was just above them. The hood had fallen from around Alice's head and now the remaining men saw her face in the fading glow of the flare.

'The Quee—'

A bullet crashed just inches from his foot, cutting his sentence short.

'I asked you a simple question. Where did you get that bag?'

The men were now shrinking back in fear. Before The Rising they had been convicts on death row, and both men were well accustomed to violence and crime; talents that had served them well in the Deadland. But for all that, they knew that they were no match for this half-Biter girl who could not be killed. They had heard tales of her and what she had done to the Red Guards, and they had given her settlement at Wonderland a wide berth, only now to be faced with her in the middle of the Deadland.

One of them gathered up the courage to speak. 'We saw a group of Biters in the Deadland a day ago. One of them dropped this.'

Alice thought back to the strange Biters she had seen at the scene of the latest attack.

'Where were these Biters going? Were they going towards the Reservation?'

The man who had spoken now looked at her curiously.

'No, that was the weird thing. We thought all the Biters around here followed you, but not these. These ones were different.'

Satish had now climbed down, but he kept his gun pointed at the two men.

'Why do you think these Biters were different?'

'They were picked up by a black helicopter.'

The next morning, Alice and Satish had the two bandits lead them to the location where they had seen the helicopter take off. Satish took a look around the area.

'Alice, if they come back, this is where they will come. They've flattened the ground to create some sort of a landing pad, and they've sandbagged those two hills to create guard towers.'

Satish got on his radio to call his recon teams. They checked in one by one, but not one of them had seen or heard a helicopter approach the area. Then again, if a black helicopter had flown in low at night, it was possible to pull off such an attack. Why and how someone would bring Biters in to launch such attacks was, however, beyond Satish.

Alice kicked the dust at her feet, thinking of the dead children back at Wonderland.

'Then we will wait here, and when they come back, we will kill them all.'

~* * * ~

'It's an attack helicopter.'

Alice heard Satish's warning and looked up to see the black, predatory shape hover in the distance. They

44

had been waiting for close to a day, and were about to give up hope and try their luck elsewhere. A makeshift bunker near the landing zone had been their regufe. They had been expecting a troop carrier, of the sort the bandit had described, and with the advantage of surprise, Alice was fairly confident that she and Satish could have handled whoever was being flown in on these deadly missions into Wonderland. However, they most certainly did not have the firepower to deal with an attack helicopter.

'How far away are your boys?'

Satish grinned. 'One of them has that chopper in his sights right now. If we order it, a SAM will be going up that chopper's tailpipe. Should we fire?'

Alice shook her head emphatically. 'No. If we show our hand now, they will not go through with their landing. Let's wait.'

But it soon became apparent this helicopter did not mean to land. It swept over the area several times, and then one of Satish's teams radioed in.

'White Rook, I can see two Red Guard APCs and two jeeps filled with Red Guards coming. Still four kilometers from your location, but they are closing in fast. Wait, they just stopped, and it looks like an officer is scanning the area with binoculars.'

Alice asked, 'What's going on?'

Satish responded, 'They seem to be on a search mission more than an attack. I have no idea what or who they might be looking for. Coming this close to Wonderland on land is a big risk for them to take, especially in broad daylight, so it must be someone important.'

Alice thought back to what she had heard in the Looking Glass. 'Could it be those Americans who had supposedly escaped?'

Satish had his own binoculars trained on the horizon and replied without shifting his gaze. 'I don't see how two escaped prisoners would warrant such a search attempt.'

Then he froze.

'Alice, look, there! At two o'clock, maybe a kilometer out, near that large Banyan tree.'

Alice had her rifle up at her shoulder and looked through the scope. It was a sunny day and there was excellent visibility, but she did not notice what Satish had seen until he pointed it out again. During her own training in the Deadland, her instructors had taught her the art of escape and evasion, but she had never really been trained to look for a concealed enemy, simply because Biter hordes were not exactly proponents of stealth and concealment. However, in the house to house fighting against the Red Guards that had followed, it had become a critical skill, one she had learnt from Satish and Arjun, and from her own combat experience.

Satish gave an appreciative whistle. 'That man sure has guts, that much is for sure. He's got an attack helicopter on top of him and perhaps fifty Red Guards on land, and he hasn't lost his nerve and made a run for it.'

Now that Alice had spotted him, she saw that there was a bit of an arm visible beneath the undergrowth. It was not going to be visible from the air, but once the Red Guard vehicles got there, it was only a matter of time before they discovered the fugitives.

Alice put her rifle aside.

'Satish, how many men do you have covering the chopper?'

'Just a two-man SAM crew and two riflemen. With the element of surprise, I have no doubt they could take the chopper down, but they cannot hold off all those Red Guards. I have two more teams with RPGs headed here, but they won't make it for the next thirty minutes.'

The buzzing sound of a large caliber automatic gun firing made Alice swivel her head around. The attack helicopter had seen something and was firing from its chin mounted turret, the rounds kicking up dust and rocks on the ground below. Alice looked through her scope and saw a frail old man stumbling along the ground. Another man was trying to pull him back under cover, but the older man had clearly lost his nerve. It was hard to be sure from this distance, but their complexion and features suggested that these were indeed the two Americans who had escaped.

She turned to look at Satish, and he just looked back, an eyebrow raised, silently asking her the question.

'Bring it down!'

As Satish relayed the order to his men, a trail of white smoke rose from the ground to Alice's left and snaked up towards the helicopter. The pilot had been so busy in trying to target the fleeing fugitives that he never had a chance to react. The missile slammed into the mid-section of the helicopter, consuming it in a giant fireball.

Alice could now see the Red Guard vehicles fast approaching the two men. She mounted the bike, with Satish behind her, and they sped towards the scene.

Alice was more than five hundred meters away when the lead Red Guard APC opened fire with its machine gun. Alice swerved her bike to the right and dove off the seat, rolling and coming up behind the cover of a large tree. Satish was concealed behind another tree. Satish's men were about a hundred meters to their left, but they too were holding their fire. Assault rifles would do little damage to the APCs.

'Over here!'

The two men heard Alice's shout and scrambled to her. Alice did not have much time to register their appearances, but they were clearly white, one a reed-thin old man whose ribs showed prominently through a dirty vest, and the other a younger man, perhaps the same age as Arjun, wearing a tattered leather jacket.

The younger man's eyes widened a bit as he saw Alice, and he started to back up, when Alice pushed him down.

'Stay here and you may just live.'

The Red Guard APCs were now advancing steadily, and they had guessed correctly that the absence of any resistance must have meant that they were not up against enemies with heavy missiles or firepower that could threaten their vehicles. The two jeeps stayed behind, and as Alice looked, an officer was standing up in the back of one of the jeeps, speaking on a radio.

'Satish, those APCs will be on us in a couple of minutes. I have a plan.'

Before Satish could say anything, Alice had reached into her backpack and taken out two fragmentation grenades and raced to her bike.

'Distract one of them!'

Satish peered out from behind cover and started firing at one of the APCs, and his men started unloading their weapons on it from the other direction. Caught in the crossfire, the commander manning the heavy machine gun on the turret was forced inside, as the other APC came towards it to deal with the sudden threat. Just then Alice's bike roared to life and she sped towards the second APC, the grenades in her hands. Distracted by Satish's men, the commander in the APC's turret did not see Alice until it was too late.

Alice pulled the pin from one grenade and threw it, jumping off her bike as it went careening into the APC. The grenade bounced off the APC and exploded, shredding several of its tires. Now the vehicle was effectively stranded, and Alice clambered onto its back, a handgun in one hand and a grenade in the other. The commander was struggling to take out his own pistol from its holster when Alice fired at him, sending him slumping back inside the vehicle. Then she pulled the pin off the second grenade and dropped it into the open hatch, jumping off as it exploded.

The Red Guards in the jeeps had now disembarked, and were firing at Alice. She felt a round hit her thigh as she sought cover behind the burning APC. The second APC was now approaching and she was effectively trapped between the dozen or more Red Guards approaching her from the right and the armored vehicle bearing down upon her from the left.

The first few Red Guards were now no more than a hundred meters away and Alice could hear their triumphant shouts as they came closer. Alice leaned out and fired a burst from her assault rifle. One seemed to go down, but there were just too many of them. And as Satish's men were pinned down by the second APC even as it drove towards her, she was on her own.

The ground near one of the Red Guards seemed to explode in a burst of dust and sand and a dark figure wearing a hat rushed up, grabbing the Red Guard and pulling him down, breaking his neck in one move. Several more Biters streamed out of the hole, overwhelming the Red Guards around them. Hatter picked up another Red Guard, raising him cleanly over his head before smashing him to the ground. Several of the Red Guards were conscripts who had never seen combat, let alone seen a Biter up close. They began to panic, and that was their undoing. They fired blindly at the approaching Biters, and while many of the scored hits, only a direct shot to the head would be of any use. Within seconds they all fell to the clawing, biting attackers who had come to Alice's rescue.

The APC now drove towards the Biters, cutting several of them into ribbons with its machine gun. The Biters were still not finished, but with their bodies mangled and their legs cut off, they were out of the fight.

Hatter was staring defiantly at the approaching APC, screaming in rage when the APC lurched to a halt, exploding from a direct hit. Alice heard Satish behind her.

'Thank God for RPGs. My boys got here just in time.'

Alice knew that they owed their survival to more than just a handful of men armed with one rocket launcher. They would not have survived without the intervention of Hatter and his fellow Biters. Several of the Biters had fallen in the battle and their bodies lay scattered around the ground, their heads blown open by direct hits.

Alice made her thanks to the surviving Biters, and then they ambled back to their hidden tunnel and disappeared. In spite of having spent so much time with them, and in spite of being like them in some respects, Alice was yet to fully figure out the Biters. They followed her with a loyalty that she had never experienced among humans, even humans who owed her their lives. They would throw away their lives to protect one of their own without a second thought, and unlike humans they never seemed to expect anything back in return. Alice was still young, but had seen enough of the world and of humans to know that those qualities were in incredibly short supply. People fought over power, over money, over control. Biters just fought to protect their own.

In becoming a Biter, it was strangely as if one became more human.

Alice's thoughts were interrupted by Satish.

'Let's now find out who our new American friends are, shall we?'

FOUR

'A JEEP WOULD be nothing more than a magnet for air strikes. Why do you think I asked all my men to disperse?'

Satish said the words with a smile, but Alice had known him long enough to recognize the underlying irritation. The two Americans had proved to be a study in contrasts. The older man, who walked with a pronounced limp, was yet to utter a word. He merely kept looking around him with wide eyes, and Alice found him staring at her way too often for her comfort. Looking at his disheveled hair, torn vest and vacant expression, she wondered if he had indeed lost his mind in some Red Guard labor camp. The younger man, conversely, was all business. He had immediately equipped himself with a bulletproof vest from one of the fallen Red Guards, and armed himself with an assault rifle. To Alice's amusement, he seemed very vocal about his opinions—though Satish certainly seemed to fine nothing funny in his trying to impose his opinion.

'How fast can we walk? Let's take one of the jeeps and get back to this city of yours.'

Satish took a step closer to the American. He was a good six inches shorter than the blond, lanky man he faced, but Alice's eyes, trained by years of experience, told her that the American would not stand a chance. He clearly had little experience of close combat, since he was holding his rifle in both hands. At such close quarters, he would never even be able to bring the rifle up before Satish cut his throat. She held out a restraining hand on Satish's shoulder and addressed the American.

'My name is Alice Gladwell. What's yours?'

'I am Captain Vince Hudson, U.S Marine Corps. I flew with the White Knights squadron before The Rising.'

He pointed to a patch stuck on his jacket, showing an armored man on horseback, carrying what appeared to be a spear or lance. Above the patch were the words 'White Knights' and below it were inscribed the letters 'HMM-165.'

'Vince, I have lived and fought in the Deadland all my life. Here are some things you should know. The Reds control the skies. So traveling in a large group is suicide. Traveling in large vehicles is suicide. And not listening to someone like Satish is suicide. We risked our lives to save you, but if you would rather be on your own, go ahead. I do not like to carry excess baggage.'

With that, Alice shouldered her assault rifle and began walking off.

'Hey, wait. Sorry if we started on the wrong foot. Being chased by Red Guards for a week has a way of putting you on edge.'

They took refuge in a nearby clump of trees. Satish had already radioed his men to give him advance warning of any incoming Red Guards, on land or by air. For close to an hour they lay flat against the ground, waiting for the telltale buzzing sound that would announce the arrival of an attack helicopter.

Finally Satish whispered, 'Looks like they've bled enough for a day. Alice, it'll be dark soon; let's get into the woods and hear what Vince and his friend have to say.'

When they were in the forest, Satish passed around a meager meal of biscuits, which the two Americans wolfed down hungrily.

Alice found the old man staring at her, and finally she turned to look at him. That was when he spoke his first words.

'You are for real. So there is hope after all.'

'Excuse me?'

The old man smiled, revealing several missing teeth.

'My name is Doctor Steven Edwards, young lady. I have a story that may interest you.'

Doctor Edwards sat back, munching on his biscuit.

'I was a virologist working for the US Department of Defense before The Rising. In the days that followed, I did what many did. I hid and survived the best I could, and one day I was picked up to go and work in some labor camp in the Mainland.'

'How long were you in the camps?' Satish asked.

'I spent eight years cleaning barracks and tilling fields. At first I tried to fight back, but when I realized there was nowhere to go to and no hope for escape, I gave in. The beatings and broken teeth helped.'

Doctor Edwards' response chilled Alice. She had heard of the camps and had talked to people who had lost relatives to them, but she had never met anyone who had survived one. She now saw the scars crisscrossing the old man's body and wondered what horrors he had endured. Having grown up to think of Biters as the ultimate horror, Alice now realized that her father had indeed been right: the worst cruelty was what man could inflict on a fellow man.

Doctor Edwards continued, 'I had resigned to slaving away in the camp until a year ago, when some folks in the Central Committee had me brought to Shanghai. They told me that they thought they could create a vaccine against the virus that turned people into Biters. Based on my background, they thought I could help.'

'Why would they single you out?'

'Because, my dear girl, I had worked on the viruses that perhaps led to this monstrosity in the first place.'

Alice thought back to the Queen of the Biters and the story she had told Alice.

'Did you know Dr. Protima?'

The old man looked down. 'I did not know her personally but I knew she was one of the researchers. Unfortunately when I did meet her, it was to harvest her dead body.'

Alice recalled how Dr. Protima had sacrificed herself in the attack to rescue Alice from the Red Guard base where she was being held. In the chaos that had followed the battle, and in wanting to escape impending Red Guard reinforcements and air strikes, Satish and his men had whisked Alice away from the base, but Dr. Protima's body had been left behind.

'I took her blood samples and got to work, thinking they were interested in only a vaccine.'

Alice explained about the vaccine Dr. Protima had given her, and Edwards looked away sadly.

'That vaccine was unstable. It saved you from becoming a Biter, but not entirely. With the labs the Reds gave me access to and blood samples from Protima, I was able to refine it.'

Satish leaned over. 'Is there a vaccine?'

'I couldn't get an actual sample out, but if I can get to a lab, I do have the details in a print-out with me. The reason we were trying so hard to get to you was that I wanted to find out if Alice was real or just a story created by people. With her blood sample and a lab I could make a vaccine that works.'

'Doctor, how did you escape?'

Vince had been silent so far, but now he chipped in. 'Not all of the Chinese are bad. As word got out about what was happening here, many of our guards were talking about whether the Biters were what they had been told. Several of them were letting prisoners escape, even against threat of execution. A young man who had lost his brother in the Deadland helped me and a few others get a spot hidden on a transport plane to Ladakh. When the doc told me what was going on, I got him along.'

'What happened to the others who escaped with you?'

The soldier's eyes hardened. 'They all died. Every single one of them. There were twenty of us, hidden among boxes of food and ammunition. We didn't have a much of a plan, but this was our best chance. When the plane landed, we tried to fight our way out. We had surprise on our side, but not much more. There were only a couple of us who knew how to use weapons, and I managed to get Doc out, but nobody else made it. We got a jeep and drove some of the way, but since then we've been walking and jacking abandoned vehicles, trying to stay alive long enough to find you.'

Something did not yet make sense to Alice.

'Doctor, why did you suddenly want to escape?'

She saw the fear in Edwards' eyes as he answered.

'They wanted a vaccine all right, but they were also doing other things. Terrible things.'

~* * * ~

Chen saw the man in front of him pace his office, his face contorted in barely controlled anger. The Commissar had flown in from Shanghai that morning, and the last time Chen had seen him was when the Central Committee was sentencing him to a labor camp. Then Chen had literally trembled in fear—but not today. The Commissar was one of the most powerful men in the Central Committee, second only to the Supreme Commander, who had not been seen in public for years. Chen had seen the worst they could do to him, and he was no longer afraid for himself, but he still had his wife to think of, so he made an attempt to placate the Commissar.

'Comrade Commissar, we lost more than two dozen Red Guards in pursuing the fugitives. It was my decision to stop the pursuit because we accounted for most of them at the airfield, but two men were not worth losing more men over.'

The Commissar turned on him, fury showing in his eyes.

'Comrade General, what were you doing before The Rising?'

The sudden question took Chen by surprise.

'I was commanding an infantry regiment.'

The Commissar stared at Chen, his eyes boring into him.

'Comrade General, I was in charge of all our strategic missile groups. You do know the decisions I had to make.'

Chen remembered the nuclear devastation that had followed The Rising and realized where Hu was going.

'So, Comrade General, difficult times call for difficult choices and sacrifice. We have sacrificed much to preserve our people and provide stability in these trying times. China is the only nation still standing from all the nations of old. More than two hundred million people still depend on the Central Committee to keep them safe. So when two fugitives escape, it is not about two people getting away; it is about people seeing that we are no longer in control.'

Hu saw a chessboard on Chen's table and walked to it, picking up a pawn.

'I realize you have been through difficult times, but we need men of your talent and experience in the coming struggle.'

Chen hesitated. 'Comrade Commissar, the war in the Deadland here has been fought to a standstill. For months, we have not aggressively pursued the terrorists, following the orders of the Central Committee.'

Hu continued to twirl the pawn in his hands.

'Comrade, any war is like a game of chess. You need to make your moves carefully, and sometimes there may be a long wait between moves. We have been patient, and we have been waiting for the right opportunity to make our move. Do you play chess, Comrade?'

Chen was getting more and more confused as to where this conversation was going.

'Comrade General, we were quiet in the Indian Deadland because we were hurting ourselves by trying to fight this Yellow Witch with conventional tactics. If anything, our men who fought in the Deadland came back with their minds filled with stories about the Biters and how the people of the Deadland had found a way of living with them. Then we had to spend time, effort and lives to re-educate them and re-instill the right revolutionary fervor. What a waste.'

Chen felt his throat tighten. He knew he was one of those who had been punished for going back to the Mainland with dangerous new questions about the war.

'Comrade General Chen, dangerous ideas like those make people question the reality that they have come to accept. The idea that they can gain so-called freedom can be a very dangerous one, for it makes people forget that in that freedom lies the loss of all the security and prosperity that we can provide.'

'With all due respect, there are enough veterans back in the Mainland who have passed on stories about the Biters and their Queen.'

Chen saw Hu smile, but there was little humor in his expression; just the look of a man who finally seemed to have things under control. He said, 'It is time we put an end to this. Time that we brought back the savages of the Deadland under our control. That is the key to stop the brimming unrest among the people of the Mainland. Once food flows onto their dinner tables and they no longer have to work on the farms, our people will stop thinking of freedom.'

'Comrade Commissar, we have tried. We brought to bear all our firepower, but you know as well as I do that in a guerilla campaign on their home ground, at best we will fight a long, hard war of attrition.'

Now Hu replaced the pawn, taking up another piece: the Queen.

'Comrade General, I flew down because I need you to know what is going on, so that you can use your experience in the Deadland and the trust your men have in you. We are about to enter a decisive phase in this battle, one that will change the game in our favor. A phase that has already begun with a few select operations behind enemy lines.'

Seeing Chen's puzzled expression, Hu pointed to the black helicopter at the far end of the base.

'Comrade General, it is time we stopped trying to win this war with pawns. The enemy has that half-Biter witch they call their Queen who they follow into battle. It's time that you met the Red Queen.'

~* * * ~

Despite all that she had seen and experienced, Alice found it hard to believe that what Edwards had shared could have happened: experiments conducted on labor camp inmates to try and create hybrid human-Biters who could wage war in the Deadland, in an attempt to create an army that would not require food, water, and be immune to pain and injury. More importantly, it would not be an army of impressionable young conscripts who would go back to the Mainland with uncomfortable questions for their masters in the Central Committee about the true nature of the war they were fighting.

Hundreds of young men and women had died in the experiments, which was when Edwards refused to co-operate any further, despite all the torture he was subjected to. When he was shipped back to the labor camp, he knew that a vaccine could be created but also knew that the Chinese researchers were getting closer and closer to their dream of creating an army of hybrids.

'That explains the Biters who attacked our people. But they seemed to move and fight like Biters, without any real human characteristics.'

Alice and Satish had brought their new companions up to speed on what they had been through. Edwards seemed to be recovering both his spirit and strength with every passing hour, as he came to grips with the fact that he was finally free.

'Satish, maybe they haven't created hybrids, but if these Biters attacked your people, and they were brought in by helicopter, the Reds have found some way of controlling them.'

Alice asked Satish to get on the radio. 'We must get in touch with Danish and get this news back. If people in Wonderland know what is happening then we can work together instead of fighting each other.'

Satish's radio came alive. Satish heard Danish's voice as he put his headset on.

'White Queen, this is Looking Glass. I have some bad news. Humpty Dumpty just sat on top of the wall. He called elections and has declared that he is the new Prime Minister. Things are pretty hot now, so suggest you not visit too soon.'

Satish slammed a fist against the ground. 'With all that's going on, Arun is still bothered about grabbing power!'

Alice sat back, wondering what she could do. It was clear that it would not be an easy job to try and get everyone in Wonderland to work together. And even more pressing, the enemy wouldn't wait until they had things together before attacking again.

~* * * ~

Chen followed Hu to the far side of the base, passing a heavily guarded checkpoint manned by black-clad Interior Security Service men before they entered the main building. The first thing he noticed was the stench, and he brought his fingers up to his nose. He saw that Hu had put on a mask covering his nose and mouth.

'Comrade General, do you want a mask?'

The last thing Chen wanted to do was to offer Hu the satisfaction of seeing any sign of weakness.

'Comrade Commissar, I have spent enough time in the Deadland to not be bothered by a bit of the smell of death. But I do wonder why a Red Guard base has been piled up with dead bodies?'

He could hear Hu chuckling as he went deeper into the building, which seemed like a warehouse with what appeared to be prison cells lining one end of it. Heavily armed black-clad guards wearing the insignia of the elite Interior Security Service stood guard. There was not a single Red Guard conscript in sight.

'Come, Comrade General. Let me introduce you to the new shock troops of the Red Army who will help us win this war and bring the Deadland back into the fold of our revolution.'

Hu guided Chen towards one of the cells, and Chen struggled to keep himself from gagging at the intense stench. When he was in front of the cell, a decayed hand with two fingers missing reached out to grab him. Chen recoiled back as a bloodied, torn face slammed into the bars.

There were more than a dozen Biters inside the cell, and many of them began screaming and banging their heads and hands on the bars. Then, just as suddenly as they had started, they stopped screaming, and to Chen's disbelief, they went down on their knees. Hu tapped him on his shoulder.

'Look this way, Comrade Chen. The Red Queen is here.'

~* * * ~

'Arun, please listen to me. We need to talk, otherwise we will have more deaths.'

Even after explaining the situation to Arun and pleading with him, Alice still faced an uphill struggle.

She had managed to get Danish to convince Arun to come to the Looking Glass. That part of the job had not been difficult at all. One of Arun's hobbies was getting time in the Looking Glass from Danish and spending hours on the radio. He had been a ham radio operator before The Rising, and while there were few people to talk to, he had actually produced a couple of very interesting connections in the short time he had been at Wonderland, including a couple of young people from the Chinese Mainland who were risking certain death or deportation to labor camps by using radios to get in touch with the outside world. From them Alice and the others had got an invaluable glimpse into what was happening inside the Mainland. They had learnt about small demonstrations and disturbances in cities like Shanghai and about how some young men had refused to be drafted into the Red Guards to be sent to the Deadland and been punished for it.

But getting Arun on the radio had been the easy part. Actually getting him to listen to what Alice had to say was proving impossible.

'Alice, thirty-four innocent people are dead, including more than twenty children. All killed by Biters, some of whose bodies we found. All this talk of Red Guards flying in Biters is fantastic but why would I not look closer to home and ask why all the Biters in the Reservation disappeared after the attacks?'

'I asked them to hide to avoid a bloodbath till we could clear things up.'

There was a pause. When Arun next spoke, Alice knew she had already lost.

'Alice, we got everyone together and had a snap election. We cannot be leaderless in this time of crisis, and I am now Prime Minister of Wonderland. I now bear the responsibility of taking care of all the thousands of people who depend on me, and I cannot act with the impulsiveness of youth that has perhaps led us to where we are.'

Alice heard Satish snort in disgust, but the last thing on her mind was bothering about barbs thrown her way.

'What if you are wrong? Do you want to risk more deaths?'

'We have strengthened our security. I have ordered all of the recon units to come back within Wonderland's borders just a couple of hours ago.'

Satish exploded at that.

'Those are my men! You cannot order them back. Without them out there, we will get no early warning about what's going on outside.'

'Satish, you no longer command anyone,' Arun replied. The civility had vanished from his voice. 'You ceased to have that privilege and trust when you helped a fugitive escape. All your trigger-happy antics achieve is to provoke the Red Guards—even more so on this latest fugitive rescue mission of yours. The last thing I want is to have your fugitives inside Wonderland and risk retaliation by the Red Guards. The bottom line is that we have known months of peace, and I do not want to risk that.'

Alice said, 'Arun, please listen to me. You spend so much time in the Looking Glass yourself. You know as well as any of us that the world outside that we see through the Looking Glass is far from being at peace.

Please give us a chance.'

'The only thing we need to talk about is you standing trial for complicity in the murder of so many innocents.' And with those final words, Arun ended the transmission.

~* * * ~

'Comrade General, meet Lieutenant Li.'

Chen took in the neatly pressed Red Guard uniform, the shoulder labels of a lieutenant, the thin and wiry frame, and then last of all, the face that stared back at him. The face of a young woman with yellowed skin, red eyes and a wound on her left cheek that had left a large chunk of her skin hanging loose. She snapped to attention and saluted.

'Comrade General Chen. It is my pleasure to be working under your command.'

When she extended her hand, Chen took it without thinking and then felt a stab of panic as he realized she was as cold as a corpse. He stepped back.

'Comrade Commissar, who is she? What is going on?'

Hu now had a smug look on his face, as Chen began to realize that he had been totally oblivious to some of the moves occurring on this chessboard of war.

Li answered, 'Comrade General, I lost my brother and my father in the war against the terrorists in the Deadland. My brother was killed in battle against this so-called Queen, this witch that the terrorists follow. I was in our Special Forces, and wanted to strike back against the enemy who had caused me so much pain. But as you well know, our tactics were of little use, and when the Central Committee asked for volunteers for a special experiment to help us strike back, I raised my hand.'

Chen studied Li, seeing not the half-Biter monster

that the scientists had somehow produced at the bidding of the Central Committee, but a young woman who had lost her family to a war based on lies. A woman who had been a good comrade, a good soldier who had never questioned the story sold to her. Was this the future? Did human salvation really lie in making monsters of us all? Was that the solution the Central Committee had to all their problems? It would surely be expedient; Biters would not ask questions and if they followed this so-called Red Queen like they followed the young girl called Alice; they would go to their deaths without any objections. It would mean not struggling for conscripts and the war could be waged in the dark, while the masses in the Mainland once again hid behind the facade of security and stability. But how would they win the war? What could one hybrid like this and a bunch of Biters really achieve?

Hu must have sensed the emotions on his face.

'Comrade General, any chess player will tell you that one piece or one move cannot be decisive. Our Red Queen has already made a couple of important moves, but we also have other pieces in play who will come into their own when the time comes. But now, Comrade General, let me tell you of what you need to do. So far we have made a few small forays but for bigger operations we will need your men to work together with Lieutenant Li and her forces, to co-ordinate our actions. Come back to your office and I will brief you on what needs to happen next.'

Thirty minutes later, Chen was back in his office. He had grown up as the son of a loyal Communist Party member and joining the Army had seemed a natural progression. He had first started questioning what he was doing when the regime started the brutal crackdowns in 2012 on popular protests in rural areas against land grabs and official corruption. That had culminated in the second bloodbath at Tiananmen Square when it had first hit home. Some of his fellow officers had dared to talk about mutiny, and Chen remembered conversations with his wife when they began to weigh their options. The Rising had changed everything. Biological attacks by the United States, regional wars and instability and retaliatory strikes by China had made everyone forget internal issues and everyone, Chen included, had rallied around the national cause.

Then came the horror of the Biters, and Chen and his fellow officers were thrown into the forefront of a terrible new war. Several months went by in a blur of savage fighting and Chen had initially been relieved when the Central Committee was formed and announced, hoping it would mean some stability and security. Securing food and safety for mainland citizens was the declared priority, and Chen signed up when the elite Red Guards were announced. Then came one revelation after another. The fact that they were to work with Zeus, an American Private Military Contractor, and then a war that soon shifted from being one waged in defense of the Mainland to an aggressive war of counter-insurgency in the Deadland. Chen had gone along, putting aside any misgivings before the terrible threat of the Biters and the need to secure food sources for the Mainland. He had directed the struggle with brutal vigor in the Deadland, with the clear understanding that the ones he was fighting were inhuman Biters and human terrorists who were disrupting the flow of food.

And then he had come face to face with Alice and the Biters, and his conviction had been shaken. He had already paid dearly for the doubts he had expressed then. What was he to do with what he had learnt today? How did one reconcile to being part of a campaign whose first salvo had included the murder of innocent children?

~* * * ~

'All but two of my recon teams are back within the city limits! I never thought they would fold so easily.'

The disappointment and hurt on Satish's face was clear. Most of his men were those he had commanded in Zeus for several years and then fought shoulder to shoulder with in the war against the Red Guards. To have them now effectively desert him and report back to the city on Arun's orders had come as a shock.

Alice was silent. She understood Satish's frustration but also knew that many of the men had wives and families back in Wonderland. They would not risk being cut off from them—but at the same time, they were now willingly blinding themselves to the Red Guards' next move. There were just two recon teams left, no more than a dozen men patrolling the vast expanse of the Deadland.

Vince was drawing something on the sand. Alice asked him what he was doing.

'We can figure out how to convince this Prime Minister of yours later. Right now, the best thing we can do is to prevent another attack. I spent the last two hours talking to Satish to understand the lay of the land and how your city is situated. I flew V-22 Ospreys in the Marines for years, so I can guess where their chopper pilots will try to come in.'

Satish radioed his teams to cover two of the likely ingress routes. He and Alice would have to cover the third. As they gathered their weapons and backpacks, they saw Vince shoulder his rifle as well. Alice looked at him and Edwards.

'You don't have to join the fight if you don't want to. This is not your war.'

She saw Vince's eyes narrow.

'Alice, this is my war. My squadron was wiped out when we refused to do what Zeus and their masters wanted, and I lost my whole family in a Red Guard missile attack.'

Alice went ahead on her bike, intending to also make contact with the Biters and get them to join the battle. The problem was that they would only follow in helping the humans if she were there to lead them. Edwards was already frail and the escape had taken a heavy toll, so he sat behind her. Vince and Satish would cover the ten-kilometer distance on foot.

Alice reached one of the nearby tunnel openings that she knew the Biters used and threw a flare down. She hoped it would be noticed in time. She was about to reach their patrol area when she felt Edwards grip her shoulder tightly.

'I can see them coming.'

FIVE

ALICE WATCHED THE two transport helicopters come in low and fast. She had not heard them until they were merely a few hundred meters away, but Edwards had seen them in the fading light. The moment she saw the helicopters, she ditched the bike and she and Edwards took cover behind a sand dune.

'I've never seen a helicopter as silent as these. No wonder they managed to come in for their attacks without us realizing it.'

Edwards peered around the dune's edge. 'Stealth, or maybe it's some sort of noise suppressant technology. The United States, China and some other countries had such technology before The Rising. Clearly they've been saving these for whatever they have in mind.'

Both helicopters landed as Alice kept watching in impotent rage. With her assault rifle and pistol, she would be able to do precious little against them. Edwards had been given a pistol, but it transpired that he'd never fired a gun before, so he would be of dubious utility in a fight. Even with Satish and Vince here they'd be hopelessly outnumbered.

The rear doors swung open on the large helicopters and Alice saw several figures walk out. From their shuffling gait it was obvious they were Biters. Alice raised her rifle scope to her eyes to take a closer look and saw what she had noticed before in Wonderland: these Biters were all wearing clean clothes and did not seem to have the many wounds and mutilations that Biters in the Deadland would almost inevitably have.

'Doctor, they seem to have produced their Biters, but one thing makes no sense to me. Biters would never follow a human being this way. How did they manage it?'

Edwards had no answer but kept watching as a total of more than fifty Biters filed out and stood there, as if awaiting orders. Alice gasped almost audibly as a woman in a Red Guard uniform walked out and the Biters knelt before her. The woman was wearing dark glasses and had her mouth covered in a mask, presumably to keep out the stench of the Biters.

'That's impossible! I've never seen Biters take orders from a human.'

Edwards' mind reeled, grappling with the science. 'I know they managed to inject healthy, loyal Chinese citizens to transform them into Biters. Perhaps they were able to create variations in the virus.'

Alice stayed focused on the assembled Biters. Their origin was unimportant; the main concern now was preventing them from reaching Wonderland. She did not fully understand what the Red Guards' plan was, but with the two Biter attacks they had effectively stripped Wonderland of much of its defenses. Alice and Satish, two of the most experienced in combat, were essentially outlaws; the Biters who had provided Alice's forces with much of its strength of numbers could no longer be counted on to defend Wonderland; and now the deep recon teams who served as their eyes and ears in the Deadland had been withdrawn to the city.

As Alice watched, the Biters began walking behind the Red Guard officer. It was less than a thirty-minute walk to the borders of Wonderland and once inside, Alice knew the kind of havoc they could wreak. The two helicopters stayed where they were, and other than the pilots there did not seem to any other Red Guards on board. That was at least one saving grace; that meant there would not be anyone to man the Gatling guns mounted on the helicopters.

Alice heard a double click on her tactical radio. That meant Satish and Vince were almost there, but she could not afford to wait. She had to do something to delay the Biters. The Red Guard officer was now striding past them, with the Biters following her, and as Alice watched the Biters began to disperse. If she didn't take them out as they were bunched up, it would be almost impossible to track them all down.

Alice took out a grenade from her belt and pulled the pin. She took a deep breath and then hurled it at the passing group. To her dismay, the Red Guard officer either had great instincts or was just very lucky. She looked up to see the dark projectile coming through the air and screamed and dove to her right. The Biters could not react with such speed and agility and as the grenade exploded, Alice saw at least three of them go down. It might not have killed them, but at least they would not move any further. The officer was now shouting orders and the Biters began to converge on her position. Edwards had his gun out and was firing, but all he managed to do was to distract them for a second before they again closed in on them. Alice now had her rifle out and was firing on single-shot mode. She took out two Biters before pulling Edwards back with her, climbing a short hill. Her only hope was to hold out until reinforcements came and to trade space for kills. She saw the Red Guard officer screaming orders and five of the Biters detached from the main group and came around from the left. Biters who could follow combat tactics on a human's orders and flank enemy positions was something Alice had never seen, but clearly this officer had some such control over them. She knelt and fired again, felling one more Biter before retreating further up the hill.

Suddenly she heard a loud roar and saw dark shapes emerge from a hole about a hundred meters to her left. Her Biters had got the message and come to her assistance. Hatter was the first out, followed by Bunny Ears and twenty more Biters. When Hatter saw the danger Alice was in, he screamed and the Biters following him tore into the attackers. Alice watched as Hatter caught one of the Biters by the neck and nearly tore his head off. Bunny Ears had only one good arm, but he and another Biter wrestled a six-foot giant down. All around Alice, Biters were locked in hand-to-hand combat, clawing and biting each other to shreds. What was clear was that Hatter and his Biters were both outnumbered and outmatched. The Biters who followed Alice had been transformed years ago, and their bodies had all the damage and wear and tear that came with being a Biter in the Deadland. The Red Guard Biters, meanwhile, were healthy by comparison, young and fit.

They were now too mixed up together for Alice to use her assault rifle, so she handed it to Edwards and took out her favored combination for close combat: knife in one hand and handgun in the other. She ran towards the melee and saw a Biter come at her from her left. A shot to the kneecap sent him stumbling down and another to the head took him out as she ran past him, barely breaking her stride. Another Biter came at her and lashed out at her. Alice was momentarily knocked off balance, but she recovered in a second, going down on one knee to avoid the next blow and stabbing up with her knife, severing the Biter's hamstring. As the Biter stumbled, she put a bullet in his head. Alice's mind was a mask of concentration, filtering out everything other than the immediate threat in front of her, and her hands and legs moved as if by their own volition, driven by years of training and combat experience.

Another Biter went down before her and then she saw the Red Guard officer. Alice saw the officer was armed with a short sword and as Alice watched, she swung it in a deadly arc, decapitating one of Alice's Biters.

Hatter was now behind the officer and Alice saw him grab the officer's arm and bite into it. Before Alice could see what happened next, a Biter came in front of her. His teeth were dripping blood and his face was torn in several places. He lunged to bite, but Alice swiped with her knife first, catching him in the throat. Before he could recover, she shot him in the face.

She paused for a second to get her bearings. It seemed that Hatter had succeeded in taking out the Red Guard officer; and without someone to control and co-ordinate them it would be easier to pick off the remaining Biters.

Alice heard a scream and looked up, and for a second her mind refused to believe what her eyes were seeing. The Red Guard officer had a large chunk of flesh torn out of her left arm but she was hardly out of the fight. No human could have been bitten by Hatter and not been affected. The officer pivoted on one leg and kicked, making solid contact with Hatter's face, stopping him in his tracks. In one fluid movement, she turned and brought her sword up and cut through Hatter's stomach, slicing upwards as she cut through his chest. The move would have killed any human, but Hatter was oblivious to pain, and the unexpected resistance only enraged him further. He tried to claw the officer's face and she swerved out of the way in the nick of time, losing her glasses and mask in the process. Before Hatter could attack again, she had cut him off at the right knee with her sword. Hatter collapsed on the ground and she brought her sword down on his head.

'No!'

Alice ran—but it was too late. Hearing her scream, the Red Guard officer stood up to face her. Now Alice was close enough to see her features and she stopped, her mind trying to reconcile to the impossibility of what she saw before her. The Red Guard smiled.

'This is an unexpected bonus. I had not hoped to meet you so soon. Now die at the hands of the Red Queen!'

~* * * ~

Alice brought up her gun to fire, but Li's hand shot out at blinding speed, and the gun flew from Alice's grip. She looked down to see a metallic star embedded in her right palm. Even before Alice had fully pulled it out, Li was upon her, screaming with her sword raised above her head with both hands. Alice brought up her knife to parry the blow and barely succeeded, the razor shap edge of the sword slicing through part of her left arm. Alice might have felt no pain, but she realized that she was up against a formidable enemy, so she rolled out of the way to gain some space and time to think.

Li's red eyes were glowering and she hissed in rage.

'I have heard much about you, Yellow Witch. Now I will avenge all you have done by cutting your head off and taking it with me.'

Alice had her knife ready, but she knew that her enemy would have a big reach advantage with her sword. She seemed to be perhaps only a few years older than Alice, and like the other enemy Biters she had seen, her face and skin seemed relatively unmarked. She came in again, thrusting with the sword, and Alice side-stepped her, twisting the knife into her stomach as she passed. As Alice regained her balance, she saw Li spit in contempt.

'You cannot gut me like a mere human, witch!'

This woman was unlike any enemy she had ever faced. Biters were simple to deal with; they knew nothing of tactics nor skill. Human adversaries, no matter how skilled or strong, were at a disadvantage versus her because they would tire, fall victim to wounds—she would not. However, for the first time she was facing someone like her, and she would have to rethink how she fought.

Li struck again and Alice again weaved out of the way, this time sweeping Li's leg under her as she passed. Li hit the ground hard as Alice turned to face the next attack. She did not know where this half-Biter had come from or where she fit into the Central Committee's plans, but one thing was clear. She was making an elementary mistake: she was fighting angry.

Li swung her sword again and grunted in despair as she missed and overshot and once again Alice stabbed her in the back before rolling away.

Li and her elder brother had been brought up in a Red Guard Academy since she had been five years old when her father had been called up on duty in the Deadland and her mother killed by Biters in the chaos following The Rising. The Central Committe had identified gifted children and trained them from an early age, hoping to create the vanguard of a new China when things stablized. As the war raged on, the graduates of the Academy became the elite officers of the Red Guards. With her impressionable young mind filled with tales of brutal hordes of Biters and of terrorists threatening the Mainland, Li had grown up with the certain knowledge that one day she too would serve her nation in this war.

Then as the war continued to rage in the Deadland and more and more Red Guard officers were rushed into frontline combat as Zeus units began to munity, her father and brother were sent to the Deadland to combat the menace posed by the terrorists led by some Yellow Witch. Rumors in the Academy spoke of a half-Biter monster who could not be killed. Then came the news that both Li's father and brother had perished in the fighting. At that time she had not yet graduated, but based on her skills had already been assigned to a Special Forces unit. She sent a petition to the Central Committee, pleading to be sent to the Deadland, hoping she would have a chance to avenge her father and brother. When Commissar Hu himself visited her and told her that she was to be part of a special unit to be inserted in the Deadland, she was ecstatic. When she learnt what she would have to endure, she began to have second thoughts. Then she was shown photos of the Yellow Witch, who it was said had been personally responsible for the death of her brother. She talked to combat veterans who told her about how her brother had been about to surrender, but had been killed in cold blood by the Witch. She was shown photographs of her brother's mutilated body. She had nobody or nothing to live for and she wanted to get revenge, so she signed up for the special program.

And now she finally had her chance at vengeance.

She was screaming at Alice to attack, but Alice held back, waiting for Li to commit to another strike. Alice knew that her only chance at a decisive blow was to the head and she would just wait for Li to make another mistake. Li had had years of the very best training. Alice had nowhere near that, but she had learned from years of living and surviving in the Deadland.

Li reached into her belt and hurled another shuriken at Alice. Alice ducked, the star whizzing past her. However that gave Li the time to rush forward with her sword, slicing deep into Alice's side. The sharp samurai sword cut into Alice's flanks where her belt was. Alice looked down and saw that it had sliced through the book she carried tied there at all times.

The sword strike would not have finished her, but she would have had a pretty hard time trying to fight with her guts spilling out, and that would have slowed her down enough for Li to finish her off. Alice backed off, thanking the storybook named after a girl called Alice for having saved her. As Li screamed in frustration and lunged at her again, Alice went down on a knee, striking up with both hands as her knife penetrated Li's defenses and took her in the chest. As Li stopped, Alice jumped up, her elbow hitting Li's nose hard. A front kick sent Li satggering to the ground.

Seeing their leader in trouble, two of Li's Biters rushed to attack Alice, who turned to face this new threat. The first Biter was just a couple of feet away when his head disappeared in a mist of blood. The second followed an instantt later. Alice turned to see Vince and Satish approaching, firing their assault rifles. The bodies of dozens of Biters lay scattered around her. While Bunny Ears and the remaining Biters were still outnumbered, with Vince and Satish there they would thin the odds pretty fast.

Li saw the new threat and knew that she would have to abort the mission. Tempting as it was to try and gain her vengeance this day, she knew that her Biters would not last against the combined force of Biters and the trained soldiers who seemed to have appeared on the scene. She screamed at her Biters to retreat and ran towards the nearest helicopter. A handful of Biters made it with her, but the others were picked off by Vince, Satish and Alice. Li looked down with rage as her helicopter took off and flew off towards Ladakh. The remaining helicopter was about to take off when Vince took aim and fired at the cockpit, killing the pilot.

Alice stood there, observing the carnage around her. They had prevented another attack on Wonderland, but at a terrible cost. She saw Bunny Ears and several of her Biters standing around

Hatter's fallen body. She had been told that Biters had no emotions, and certainly they could not cry, but there was no doubting that Bunny Ears and the others had felt something at the passing of their comrades.

Edwards ventured from cover.

'Now I know what they were after with their experiments. They wanted to make another like you, and looks like they succeeded.'

Alice saw Vince grinning. She raised her eyebrows; what could he possibly find funny in the middle of all this bloodshed? He saw her expression and while his grin instantly disappeared, there was no mistaking the excitement in his eyes. He pointed to the helicopter the attackers had left behind.

'Look at the bright side. Now we have our own air force.'

~* * * ~

Chen cringed as he heard the sounds of the neighboring office being trashed. When only one helicopter had come back, he had known something was wrong, and Li had rushed into the office in a rage. He looked at Hu.

'Comrade Commissar, she seems like a spoilt young girl, not your elite super soldier.'

He noted with some satisfaction the twitch of irritation on Hu's face, but the Commissar quickly recovered his composure.

'Give her some time. In the meantime we will go and sit in your office.'

They passed the time with chess. Chen thought he had the Commissar on the ropes when he managed to trap the Queen, but then Hu surprised him by checkmating him within two moves. The normally humorless Hu allowed himself a smile as he spoke.

'Comrade General, sometimes one must turn defeat into victory. Did you see the piece I used to distract you?'

'Yes, Comrade Commissar, you made me think you had left your White King vulnerable.'

Hu got up and walked to the window, watching the building at the far end of the base, where Li was probably still taking out her anger on the office furniture.

'Comrade General, I did not anticipate that they would intercept this mission, but perhaps there is yet something we can salvage from this. These is one other possibility; a White King I have been using for small moves. Perhaps now his role can become more decisive.'

~* * * ~

Danish was in front of his console in the Looking Glass. He had got word of the battle and while Alice had not told him the full story, since their communications were most likely intercepted by the Red Guards, the mention of a Red Queen and her Biters had him worried no end. If the Red Guards had been behind the Biter attacks, they had at one stroke found a way of driving a wedge between the humans and Biters in Wonderland and depriving Wonderland of some of its most experienced fighters.

Arjun came up behind him.

'Danish, I have a Cabinet meeting with Arun in the evening, so I thought I'd check if you needed anything from town.'

Danish asked Arjun to sit down.

'I don't know how you do it. You must not just have been a salesman, but a bloody Oscar winning actor before The Rising. You actually have Arun convinced that you're going to side with him.'

Danish had spoken in jest, but Arjun's reply was dead serious.

'When the time comes. Till then, I can't have all of

us desert Wonderland. Any news from the Americans?'

The question brought a smile to Danish's face.

'Oh yes! They've got several servers up, and while the Red Guards are trying to block them, they are now communicating a lot with each other and with us over the Net. The news is that they've re-captured a couple of old airbases. After so many years, I have no idea if they can get those planes flying and combat ready, but if they do, then the battle for the American Deadland will be really interesting.'

Arjun asked him what he was planning for lunch, and Danish replied, patting his ample belly, 'I haven't had breakfast, so let's get to town and grab a bite at McDonald's.'

McDonald's was the name given to the first and so far only restaurant in Wonderland. It had been opened in the burned out shell of an old restaurant from before The Rising, but the large yellow 'M' had survived and while the food served consisted of soups, rice, vegetables and the occasional burger when hunting parties got lucky, it made everyone feel better that they had the option to eat in a restaurant again. It was one small step on the long and winding road towards normality.

A jeep pulled up outside and they saw Arun walking in.

'Hey, Arun. I'm stepping out for lunch. The Looking Glass is all yours.'

Arun sat down and fiddled with the radio in front of him. He had never anticipated that this hobby of his from before The Rising would prove so handy now. He had been a member of parliament, one of the rising young stars of Indian politics, when The Rising took place. People had said that he would one day have a shot at being Prime Minister, that he was destined for great things. The Rising had changed all that. At one stroke, he had gone from a man of considerable power and influence to one who was nothing. After The

Rising, the only people who really counted were those who were strong enough or ruthless enough to survive the chaos that followed. Arun had gone into hiding in the Ruins with his family, and seen two children be taken by the Biters. They had stumbled into a settlement in the Deadland where they had lived the lives of scavengers, sending a few young boys and girls every month with Zeus troopers to serve in labor camps or farms for a modicum of security. He had been happy when Alice had emerged, leading her rebellion against the Central Commitee. He and his family had walked into Wonderland just over a year ago, but quickly his relief at returning to a more stable, safe existence had given way to mixed emotions. How could he tolerate the fact that they were supposed to now live in peace with Biters, the same monsters who had taken his children? How could he look at Alice every day, and follow the half-Biter monster she had become? Not having any alternatives, he had been content to serve for some time, and his skills with the ham radio were well appreciated, but one day he got a transmission that told him that he perhaps had a chance after all to realize the future he once believed he was destined to achieve. He tuned into the right frequency and awaited his instructions.

~* * * ~

Edwards was holding the charred and torn book in his hands with an almost reverential air. Alice had seen Dr. Protima behave that way, but that had been because she had believed that the book contained a prophecy Alice was destined to fulfil. For Edwards, there were different emotions at work.

'Alice, when people talk of starting off on civilization again, they look at buildings, at electricity, at running water. All of those are important, but what they forget is that perhaps the most important thing to start over may be now in my hands.'

'What does that mean?'

'Our minds react to things as we see them, and usually with our basest instincts of fear, hatred and self-preservation. But a book captures the best of what people can be. A book reminds us of what is possible when we put those baser instincts aside. The ability to create something that will last beyond us, and carry our ideas to the next generation. When you get back to Wonderland, you must get them to start making books again.'

Alice played with the grass at her feet.

'I don't know when and how we'll ever get back to Wonderland. I had thought that with peace we would get a chance to create a better future.'

Edwards smiled. 'It is easy to make peace with an enemy, but difficult for ambitious men to make peace with their own greed and hunger for power. From what you've told me, that is what led to The Rising in the first place. It looks like man hasn't really learnt any lessons from it.'

Ever since the battle, Alice's mind had been on litle else other than the unexpected adversary she had just faced.

'Doctor, do you think that you can really create a vaccine that works?'

'Science can always be used for good or evil. The Central Committee is perhaps keen on creating an army of hybrids, but that same science can be used to not just create a vaccine to prevent infections among humans, but perhaps cure Biters as well.'

That made Alice straighten. 'Do you think the Biters can be cured?'

'I'm not sure, but looking at their behavior closely, I can say that they are more than just brutes. Yes, there must be some brain damage, but at the very least if we can curb their aggressive instincts, it would make coexistance much easier.'

Alice remembered what she had heard from Danish about what has happening in the American Deadland.

'Have people always reacted with so much hatred to those different from them?'

Before Edwards could reply they saw the helicopter come back for a landing. Vince had been like an excited child when he saw the prospect of flying again, and he and Satish had taken off in the captured helicopter for a quick reconaissance flight. As the helicopter landed, and Satish slipped out and ran toward them.

'Alice, Arun doesn't know how big a mistake he made by having our recon teams pull back. We barely flew out a hundred kilomteres and I could see more than a dozen Red Guard APCs on the roads. This is the first time in months they've come out in such numbers..'

Vince was soon with them as well. His eyes danced with excitement.

'I thought I would never be able to fly again. When I was up there, it felt like I could once again make a difference, that I could once again be worth something.'

Satish slapped him on the shoulder, and Alice could tell that the earlier frostiness between the men had gone. Though she was still young, she knew that there was little that bonded two people more than being in combat together.

'Alice, the Red Guards will slowly but surely start taking control over the outlying areas. If they do, you know how easy it will be for them to form a chokehold over Wonderland. Thousands died so we could have this freedom, and now we risk losing all that to petty politics.'

At that, Edwards scoffed. 'It's an old truth. In any war, the soldiers and common people bleed, and the politicians rule over the rubble that remains.'

A few minutes later, Satish came running to Alice.

'It's Danish on the radio. He says that Arun and his so-called Cabinet have voted and they want us to return. He says that Arun wants to talk to us and has a proposal he wants to put before us.'

Alice exhaled deeply in relief.

'Thank whichever god anyone still cares to believe in that Arun has some sense after all. Let's get back to Wonderland. Once we get the doctor and Vince in front of them they will have to believe our story about the Biters being sent in by the Red Guards.'

Satish was not so easily reassured. 'Alice, I don't trust Arun one bit. This could just be a trap. For all you know, he's calling us back to arrest us and put us up in front of some court where he acts as judge, jury and executioner. I want to call my remaining recon boys in so they can go with us.'

Vince tapped Alice on the shoulder. 'We will ride in at a place and time of our choosing. And if there's trouble, we can always fly away.'

Within an hour they were joined by eight of Satish's men who were still patrolling the Deadland and the captured helicopter took off, its destination the old airport on the outskirts of Wonderland.

SIX

A LICE NOTED WITH some disappointment that the old airport did not have any guards posted near it. The runway was still functional and with stealthy helicopters like these, the Red Guards could have landed a few hundred men there without Arun and his politician friends even knowing about it.

When their helicopter landed, Satish ordered his men to fan out and guard the entry points to the airport. The Red Guards had made extensive use of the airport to fly out labor for camps in the Mainland and to fly in supplies for their forces in the Deadland, so the defensive bunkers near the main gate were still there. When Alice checked, the gun turrets the Red Guards had abandoned after the airbase had been overrun by Alice and her forces still worked. When Satish was satisfied that they were in a defensible position, he got on the radio to Danish.

'Looking Glass, this is White Rook. I have the White Queen with me and we've flown in to pay a little visit to Humpty Dumpty.'

The mention of 'flying in' gave a surprised edge to Danish's voice, but he sent a jeep to come meet them, Arjun at the wheel. He ran towards Alice, relief apparent on his face.

'Thank God you guys are all okay. I was so worried

about you being out there without much back-up. Danish filled me in on the battle but what really is going on?'

When Alice and Satish had debriefed him, they saw that Arjun looked quite worried.

'I don't know whether Arun and his friends will want to believe that the Red Guards were behind the Biter attacks. He wants to sign a treaty with them.'

Alice was dumbfounded.

'After all we've been through, does he really believe that we can make peace with the Central Committee?'

Arjun came close to her so that the Americans would not hear him.

'Alice, are you sure you want to take Vince and the doctor in to meet Arun?'

'Of course, Arjun! He may not believe me but they have just escaped from the Reds and both of saw the battle against the Biters the Red Guards flew in. They're our best chance of convincing Arun that what we're saying is the truth.'

Less than an hour later, Arun arrived at the airport for the meeting. He wore a bemused expression on his arrival at the defenses they had set up.

'Alice, surely you do not think I will try and attack all of you on my own?'

Satish cut in, 'Given how much trust you have shown in us and the fact that there has already been an attempt on Alice's life, we thought we'd prefer to meet on our terms.'

Arun looked at Satish with a trace of irritation— and then he was all business again, his smile back.

'Come on. Let's meet inside. I have much news to share with you.'

'Yes, Prime Minister.'

If Arun was irked at Satish's sarcasm, he didn't let it show.

Inside, Vince and Edwards related their stories to Arun. When they had finished, Arun looked straight at Alice.

'I have heard all you had to say. Now, for the sake of Wonderland, hear me out. The Central Committee has proposed a treaty.'

Alice cut him off. 'How can we even think of a treaty with them after all we've been through?'

'There was a time for war and warriors, and people like you and Satish did more than anyone could have asked of you in serving our people. Now it is a time for peace and for statesmen, and I know more of that world than you do. No enemy or ally is permanent, but only our interests are. If Wonderland is to survive, we must learn to adapt and forget past enmities.'

'What do you have in mind?'

Arun held up a tablet that had a message from the Central Committee. Someone called Commissar Hu had signed it. Alice scanned it, the disbelief in her voice clear when she spoke.

'Arun, how can we take their demands seriously? They ask us to stop aggressive actions in the Deadland when they are the ones attacking and provoking us. They ask us to stop all contact with the Biters when you know how much we owe the Biters in our war against the Red Guards. They ask us to open trade routes when you know that means that they will take what they have always wanted: labor to work their camps and farms to feed the Mainland. What do we get in return?'

'Legitimacy. Alice, let's face it; the world is in ruins and the only nation still standing is the Chinese mainland. They would recognize us as another nation, and commit to a ceasefire. We would get access to their technology; our people would stop scavenging for food and bare necessities. We could once again start afresh as civilized people.'

'Does having the comforts of so-called civilized living ever make up for the loss of freedom?'

Arun was now almost pleading with her. 'Alice, stop

thinking in absolutes. You were born after The Rising, but before that nations fought great wars and then worked together driven by pragmatism. We can do the same.'

Alice stared. There was nothing she could say to convince him.

'My father used to say that our willingness to defend compromises with tyrants as pragmatism is what has led to our ruin time and again. We cannot compromise with the Central Committee.'

Arun sighed. He took the tablet back and said, 'I was trying to convince you because there are still people in Wonderland who look up to you, and I know how much you have sacrificed for the people here, but I am not asking for your permission. I am the elected Prime Minister of Wonderland and I have already agreed to the terms the Commissar wanted.'

'Did you even listen to what Vince and the doctor had to say? Those attacks that killed our children were carried out by Biters created by the Reds.'

'Yes, the attacks were committed by Biters, but there is no evidence that the Red Guards sent them, and as for your last battle, there is no proof of what you say other than your own testimony—and we both know you have a vested interest in making your precious Biters appear clean.'

'So why did you want us to come here? What do you want of me now?'

'You have a clear choice. Stay with us in Wonderland and abide by the new rules and I'll ensure that people don't pin any blame on you for the Biter attacks. If not, you will be evicted from Wonderland and I'll ensure that the Central Committee knows that Wonderland has nothing to do with you and your actions.'

Alice could feel Satish reaching for his gun, but she placed a hand on his arm. So it had finally come to this. After all she had done and sacrificed, she was to be sold out in a political compromise. Part of her told her to fight the decision, but she knew that even if she managed to convince some of the people in Wonderland, more than enough of its residents would side with Arun. The only thing worse than a false peace with the Central Committee would be open civil war in Wonderland.

Satish pulled her aside.

'Alice, you cannot seriously be considering what he says.'

When Alice spoke, she could not look at him. 'If we go on our own, what will the handful of us achieve in the Deadland? We cannot free those who want to be enslaved. Our best bet is to be in Wonderland so that when the time comes, we can at least be of use here.'

Satish was furious—but deep down, he knew Alice was right.

~* * * ~

Back at the Ladakh airbase, Chen could see the smirk of satisfaction on Hu's face as he listened to the barrage of complaints from Li.

'Comrade Commissar, send me out again. This time I will smash that White Queen and her forces! How can we make peace with those terrorists?'

'Comrade Li, not every war is to be won with brute force alone.'

But that only made Li grow more agitated, so Hu stepped closer with a conciliatory wave of his arms.

'Comrade, your raids served their first purpose. The people of Wonderland have a new leader, one we can work with. They no longer simmer in open resentment of us under the banner of the Yellow Witch. There will be once again a time when you and your troops take to the battleground. For now we will open a new front in this war.'

'What do you mean, Comrade Commissar?'

Hu looked at Chen with a broad smile.

'Comrade General, our next battle will be one based on lessons we ourselves learnt well in our history. We will smother them with our kindness, and in that dependence will be born the seeds of our ultimate triumph over these savages.'

~* * * ~

Even compared to when the Red Guards had captured her, Alice had never felt so imprisoned. At least then her status as a prisoner was clear and she knew that, given half a chance, she would try and fight her way to freedom. Now she was bound by invisible straps. Instead of physical chains her shackles lay in the fact that she was helpless and powerless to help those she most cared about. She knew that the only way she could still help the people of Wonderland was to be one of them, not an outlaw in the Deadland. So she stayed in her room and watched as Wonderland changed around her.

The first sign of what was to come was Danish radioing her to tell her that the Central Committee had issued a message aimed at not just the citizens of its Mainland but also the people of Wonderland. The message said that after much conflict and bloodshed caused by terrorists and counter-revolutionaries, the democratically elected government of Wonderland had reached out to establish peaceful relations with the Mainland. The Central Committee welcomed this move, as it believed that the last two remaining bastions of human civilization needed to work together and forget past misunderstandings. It apologized for the violence that had been caused by terrorist leaders and renegade Zeus officers and pledged to bring about a new era of prosperity for the people of Wonderland. It went on to claim that the government of Wonderland had pledged to not give refuge to Biters.

To Arun's credit, he had not tried to defend all that the statement had said, but in the Council building where this had been discussed he had said that the Central Committee was catering to its own domestic audience. Looking at him addressing the large crowd and seeing how they seemed to lap up what he said, Alice learnt an important lesson: people got the leaders they deserved simply because people tended to follow those who projected their own fears and aspirations.

That afternoon, she had an unexpected visitor in the form of Arun.

'Alice, I hope you are doing well.'

She had no interest in exchanging pleasantries, so went straight to the point. 'Looks like your plan for Wonderland is well underway.'

'No, Alice, it's not my plan alone. It is our plan. We all share in the success of this plan for we will all reap the benefits. Don't you see that by signing this treaty we have brought peace?'

'Arun, do you really believe we will achieve peace?'

Smiling smugly, Arun said, 'Don't think I spent all those hours in the Looking Glass only fiddling with my ham radio. I've seen all the Intranet reports, including the ones the Central Committee pulls down after a few hours. The war here is very unpopular back in the Mainland as well, with people asking why their young men are being sent to die in the Deadland for no real gain. With this announcement, the Central Committee has effectively announced an end to the war here. They will not be able to undertake any large scale military operation without it totally losing them support back home.'

At that moment, Alice saw Arun in a new light. She had believed that he was pushing for the plan only because he wanted power for himself. And perhaps that was part of it, but it was clear that he had thought it through and genuinely believed that he was doing what was best for the people of Wonderland. It was as Danish had said: the road to Hell was paved with good intentions.

Alice did not want to spend much time in the city center where she kept catching people staring at her, some looking at her with scarcely contained hatred and others asking a question with their eyes that they dared not say aloud: why was she silent? The ones who had been with her from the beginning, the ones who had felt the brunt of the fighting, felt that all they had fought for was being given away. But some of her early supporters had been shaken by the Biter attacks, and were no longer sure whom to believe any more. And then there were the more recent arrivals like Arun, who did not owe much personal allegiance to Alice but wanted to create Wonderland in their own vision.

Alice rode her bike to the outskirts, passing the abandoned Biter Reservation. On her instructions, Bunny Ears and the others had gone underground, but Alice had clearly felt their sense of betrayal. She did not doubt that Bunny Ears would remain loyal, but many others, once more wild in the Deadland, and perhaps hunted by the Red Guards, would again grow to hate and fear man.

She entered the Looking Glass to find Danish with Edwards and Vince. The two Americans had taken to spending most of their days at the Looking Glass, perhaps because it was the one way they could get a glimpse into what was happening back in their homeland.

'Alice, come over here. The Americans seem to have more servers up and running and there are several webpages now active. Some seem to have disappeared—I think the Central Committee is fighting to block them—but there are some that we can see.'

Alice quickly scanned through what the pages told her. The story they depicted was one very familiar to her, since she herself had lived through such a tale.

The Americans were now waging their own war for freedom, much as Alice and her friends had waged in the Deadland. The reports she read spoke of terrible house-to-house fighting in the abandoned shells of what had once been mighty cities, of Red Guard missile strikes that killed hundreds of women and children, and of the continued menace of Biters. The Americans were fighting hard but they had two things going against them. First, with the relative peace in the Indian Deadland, the Central Committee had been able to divert its elite combat-tested units to the American Deadland, leaving the Indian Deadland to a few conscripts. Second, in the American Deadland, man and Biter were still locked in a struggle for survival.

Alice could see the expression on Vince's face, and she wasn't sure she wanted to answer the questions she knew he would have for her. However, it was Edwards who spoke.

'Alice, I can understand why Arun and the others have made the choices they did, but Vince and I need to leave.'

'Why? Where will you go? I thought you wanted to seek us out in the first place.'

Vince got up, looking out the glass windows.

'We were trying to find a place that had become almost legendary among American prisoners. A place where ordinary people were finally fighting back to regain their freedom. A place where a young girl had united humans and Biters in trying to overthrow the tyrants of the Central Committee. This is no longer that place. I cannot sit here and watch as fellow Americans fight and die while the place that inspired their struggle in the first place surrenders to the Central Committee.'

Alice didn't know what she could say or do. She had never felt so helpless before.

'Vince, how do you think I feel? But I cannot

abandon these people or Wonderland. I trust the Central Committee even less than you do, but the only way I can really help my people is to be here when I am needed.'

Edwards placed a reassuring arm on Alice's shoulder.

'Alice, Arun is playing a dangerous game. If there is one thing history teaches us, it is that one can never reach a compromise with tyrants, for they inevitably mistake any concessions for weakness. The Central Committee will be plotting and I fear that in marginalizing you and your friends, and in creating a rift between human and Biters once more, they will have gained a critical advantage when they do move against you. I wish you all the best, but I am of little use here. I need a lab to work on my vaccine and Arun will not permit me one. I need to find a way back to America, and perhaps one day we can find a cure.'

Before they could talk any further, Danish tapped on the screen.

'It's a new message from our friend Commissar Hu. The Central Committee is sending a plane-load of goods as a gesture of friendship towards their fraternal brothers of Wonderland.'

Alice knew she had to get Satish, and fast.

~* * * ~

Without their recon teams deep in the Deadland, they would get little advance warning of what exactly the Central Committee was up to. Alice could see that even Arun looked anxious. A lot was at stake, and if the Central Committee were to launch an airborne assault, it would undo everything. But Alice knew they would be far from defenseless. Within hours, Satish had a plan in place. His men were ringing the airport and the outlying areas, armed with SAM launchers. At any sign of trouble, they would shoot down the Red

Guard aircraft. Vince had taken off in the captured helicopter to give them some advance warning of what was coming their way, and Arjun had gathered his internal security teams to be ready for any eventuality.

All of Wonderland was on tenterhooks, and Alice and Arun were standing near the airport when Vince's voice came in over the radio.

'It looks like a single transport aircraft. I can't see any signs of other air or ground forces.'

Arun's relieved sigh was audible.

Within minutes, they saw the faint outline of the approaching aircraft. Despite the fact that it was one airplane, Alice felt herself tense. Red Guard aircraft brought back memories that she wished she did not have, memories of the air strike that had killed her mother and sister and the other survivors from her settlement, and of the strikes that had been launched against Wonderland when she had been captured.

The black plane banked to its right and then came in, heading for the runway.

Alice saw Satish signal to one of his teams and she knew that even as the aircraft approached, several missiles would have locked in on it.

The aircraft landed bumpily on the old runway and came to a rolling halt. Flanked by several men, Arun approached the plane as the ramp behind the aircraft lowered and a solitary man walked out. Alice looked through her binoculars and saw that he was a young officer dressed in the uniform of the Red Guards. He saluted Arun and then offered his hand, which Arun shook. Then he pointed inside the aircraft and motioned to someone inside.

As Alice watched, Red Guards brought out several dozen large crates, which they left on the runway. As she watched, one of them opened a crate and Arun peered inside. She saw a smile form on his face and wondered what the Red Guards had brought with them. Within minutes, the crates had been moved to the side of the runway and the plane had taken off and returned to its base.

If anybody found it ironic that trucks captured from Red Guards killed in battle were being to transport these gestures of goodwill from the Central Committee, they kept their opinion to themselves. All the crates were brought into a field near the Council building and a huge crowd had gathered in no time, jostling to see what they contained.

Up until now, Arjun had been silent, but now he pulled Arun and Alice aside. Arun bristled a bit at having to share decision making with Alice, but a sideways glance from Arjun shut him up.

'Arun, let me and my men inspect all the crates thoroughly. Only when we are sure that they are safe should we let people get at them. Also, the last thing we need is a stampede, so get these people home and tell them that we'll sort through what's been sent and get back to them tomorrow.'

Arun agreed and the orders were soon passed out, and most of Wonderland spent that night in eager anticipation of what they would find in the crates the next morning.

~* * * ~

'Alice, I am requesting you to help us. All we need is a small sign from you. We have more than a dozen old combat aircraft almost operational and every day we are bleeding the Red Guards dry. Our battle for liberation got a second life thanks to you and your struggle in the Deadland, but now the Red Guard propaganda says you have surrendered. They are dropping leaflets saying that Wonderland has accepted the Central Committee's terms. Just issue a statement saying it isn't so.'

'General Konrath, please give me some time to think things over.'

Alice was seething with frustration and anger at her helplessness. The American General was not asking for much, but Alice knew that having accepted Arun as the leader of Wonderland and having decided to play along with the treaty, she could not even do that much.

Vince said from beside her, 'Alice, it would be easy. There was a webcam on board the helicopter we captured. Danish and I could rig it up and we could upload your message to one of the American servers.'

Danish slammed his fist onto the desk in frustration. 'We could, but then Arun would go crazy. He comes here every day supposedly to twiddle with the radio, but I know he's keeping tabs on what we do.'

Alice was looking at the screen.

'It's not just Arun and what he may think. The Central Committee would certainly see this as an act of war, and they would react.'

Danish looked up at her. 'Alice, since when you have been worried about what the Central Committee may or may not think?'

Alice walked out, a bitter tinge to her voice as she replied, 'I was always happy to fight to the end. But I had people I could count on, people I knew would fight by my side. How does one fight to free people who have come to like the comfort of slavery?'

~* * * ~

Chen was sitting in his office, which had been shifted to the warehouse, and which he now shared with Li. He hated her stench, but then he had not been given any option in the matter. The one saving grace was that Li was usually out training most of the day, at the firing range or practicing close combat with her Biters. Their presence at the base was still secret, and when he went back to the cafeteria in the main building for meals he would get questioning glances from his young conscripts—questions he could not answer. Hu had expressly forbidden him from revealing the real identity of Li and her Biters. The official line, which Chen parroted, was that they were a secret Special Operations unit flown in from the Mainland. He knew he would have got many uncomfortable questions had the peace treaty not been announced. At least there was to be no more fighting in this accursed war. Chen had no idea what Hu and his masters in the Central Committee were planning, but he just hoped that he could go back home and no longer have to stain his hands with the blood of innocents; both his young men and the civilians of Wonderland.

He saw a video conference call incoming on his tablet. It was Hu.

'Greetings, Comrade General. Our token of goodwill has reached the people of Wonderland. When the time is right, I will have another shipment for them.'

Chen was a career soldier, and understood the cut and thrust of combat, but he had no idea what political machinations lay behind Hu's latest moves.

'Comrade Commissar, dare I ask what we plan to do after that and what the orders for my men are in terms of combat readiness?'

He could see Hu smile and share a glance with someone off camera. No doubt some political officers were on hand to judge if Chen's revolutionary fervor was intact or not.

'Comrade General, we are still very much at war. The people's revolution cannot be sustained as long as counter-revolutionary forces spread the lie of democracy in savage places like Wonderland. The false idea of democracy died in the flames of The Rising. Our people need to know that there is only way to assure stability and progress, and that is for us to join together under the benevolent guidance of the

Central Committee.'

Chen's eyes were glazing over. A year ago, he might have been more tolerant of such propaganda, no doubt uttered for the benefit of the political officer watching Hu, but months of torture and 're-education' in the camp had left Chen with little patience for such platitudes. Hu looked at him, a new hard glint in his eyes.

'Comrade General, do you remember our own history and how we were so addicted to opium that we did not see the occupiers for who they really were? The people of Wonderland will learn a similar lesson, but it will be too late for them to do much about it.'

~* * * ~

The opening of the crates attracted thousands of people, and Arun triumphantly stood on stage displaying what had been sent as if this were yet another vindication of his decision. Alice was accompanied by Arjun and Satish, their contempt scarcely disguised on their faces.

Each crate had two lines stenciled on its side in large red letters:

'For our brothers and sisters in Wonderland.'

'Made in China.'

When the first crate was opened, Arun took out what seemed to be a bunch of plastic toys. Brightly colored cars, stuffed animals, and dolls in frilly dresses. Alice could hear gasps in the audience and more than one child demanded to take a closer look. Growing up in the Deadland, Alice had never really had the luxury of toys, but had heard about how children before The Rising had played with them. Seeing these bright new toys made her think of all she had missed and would never really have. Even in the relative stability of Wonderland, the best any family had managed was to fashion its own crude toys from scavenged items. For the parents of the children gathered in front of the stage, many of whom had wished they could give their children a real child's life instead of one filled with death and violence, there was no mistaking the excitement in their eyes and voices.

The buzz of excitement was renewed when the second crate was opened. Inside were fresh clean clothes, a blackboard and chalk for the school, plates and cutlery, and finally a huge supply of canned meat and food that Arun declared would form the new menu at McDonald's. At one stroke, Wonderland had regained many of the comforts that most of its inhabitants had almost forgotten.

The last crate contained the biggest prize of all: a large, slim screen.

'It's a TV,' whispered Satish.

Alice had never seen a TV before, and Arun read out some instructions that came with the TV, saying that there would be a daily broadcast for the people of Wonderland in the evening.

That evening, almost all of Wonderland gathered in front of the large TV, and there were squeals of delight as the programming began. There was a children's cartoon, something about a mouse Alice had never heard of, and then something that Satish called a rerun of an old soap opera, which to Alice merely seemed to be overweight and painted women flirting with men. But to the gathered crowd it seemed to be a miracle. For more than fifteen years none of them had watched TV, and they sat glued to it, including the ten minute capsule after the soap opera that consisted of propaganda from the Central Committee about how the 'people's revolution' was restoring prosperity and civilization.

The next day, Alice and Edwards were strolling down the main street, watching people queue up outside McDonald's for a taste of the canned meat, when they spied two young boys fighting over a plastic car. Edwards shook his head sadly.

'We never learn. Once more we sell our ideals for cheap plastic toys.'

SEVEN

THE FOLLOWING DAYS fell into a predictable routine. Most people at Wonderland would line up at McDonald's for lunch and dinner, and soon Arun found himself having to ration the stocks that had been sent. The people of Wonderland wore better clothes than they had in years and when one of the crates was found to contain bottles of shampoo and bars of soap, a small riot had almost erupted to divide up the spoils. Alice was riding her bike by the school and she saw a group of children walk by, all freshly scrubbed, wearing bright clean clothes and carrying new toys. She remembered her own childhood spent hiding and fighting in the Deadland, taking a bath once in a week, and wearing the same clothes until they wore out. She stopped to see the laughing children and wondered if Arun had been right after all. The Central Committee was certainly not demanding that people be sent to work in labor camps and so far they had made no aggressive moves towards the borders of Wonderland. Was peace with the Mainland indeed possible?

While Arun and his supporters reveled in their newfound comforts, Alice found herself totally out of place in this new world. The only life she had known had been one of fighting to survive. With no war to fight, how did warriors fit back into a society that had passed them by?

Arjun was hardly happy with the way Arun had compromised with the Central Committee, but he was too busy maintaining order within Wonderland. New clothes, toys and the TV meant that people had more things to covet and fight over. Satish sat brooding in the Looking Glass with Danish most of the time. He, like Alice, had defined himself by the war he had been fighting, and now he was just as out of place as her. Many of his men had wives and families in Wonderland and quickly lapsed into civilian life, but Satish stayed at the Looking Glass, his soldier's instinct telling him that this peace was to be ephemeral.

Meanwhile, Vince and Edwards were plotting in their own unique ways.

Vince had taken to spending most of his time tinkering with the captured helicopter, which he guarded jealously. Alice rode by the airfield, hoping to find someone to talk to. Vince was loading the helicopter up with cans of fuel.

'Hi, Vince. What are you doing?'

Vince wiped the sweat from his brow.

'Alice, there's a war on, and if the people of Wonderland are going to ignore it, then I may as well try and get to America and join up with our forces there.'

'How on earth will you get there? It's the other side of the world.'

Vince tapped inside the cockpit. There was a small computer, its screen covered in numbers and letters.

'This bird has a pretty good navigational system and a computer that uses old GPS co-ordinates. Wait until General Konrath and the others find out that some of the old GPS satellites are still operational. We could sure use some of that technology.'

Alice looked back at Vince blankly; she had no idea

what he was talking about.

Vince explained, 'I've run the calculations. This bird can fly about 3000 kilometers one way on its internal fuel and the external tanks if I fly slow and easy. If I carry some extra fuel with me, I may be able to stretch that by five hundred kilometers or more. I'll have to stop along the way since I can't fly that long non-stop, but I could feasibly reach Thailand or Israel in a couple of days, depending on the direction I fly. Given that the Middle East is still stewing in its radioactive juices, my best bet may be to fly east.'

He took out a map he had found in the cockpit and showed it to Alice. It was the first time Alice had seen a map of the world and she was both fascinated by both the world's vastness, and the tiny insignificance of their minute patch of land.

'Vince, even if you make it to this place called Bangkok, your home in America is still far away across the ocean. How will you get there?'

Vince put away the map and grumbled. 'I'm still working on it, but I am not going to sit around here and become a slave to the Central Committee all over again.'

Alice's next stop was the Looking Glass. Danish and Satish had stepped out for a breath of fresh air and she found Edwards inside. He was furiously tapping away on the keyboard. When he heard Alice enter, he quickly turned around to see who was there.

'Thank God, it's just you.'

'What are you doing, Doctor?'

Edwards pointed to the screen, on which he had written a seemingly incomprehensible sequence of letters. On the table in front of him was a crumpled and dirty piece of paper that he seemed to be copying the letters from.

'I don't know if I will ever get back to America or not, but I don't need to be there physically to share some of what I've learnt. As Danish would have told you, we're restoring many of the old servers there and many websites have cropped up. Many of them are being used to pass messages between the resistance forces there, but I found that at least a couple of my old colleagues are still alive and well. I had written down some of the things I had learnt about the structure of the virus in the Central Committee's labs and am posting on a message board one of my old colleagues in America had visited.'

'Doctor, could they make a cure or vaccine with that information?'

Edwards shook his head.

'No, they would not be able to do that with this alone. To do that they would need a real blood sample, but at least all this knowledge will not be lost.'

He pressed a key and sat back.

'Well, that's gone now. What news of Wonderland?'

Alice sat down. 'I don't know how to describe it. People seem happier than I've ever seen them. They've got better food, cleaner clothes, the children have real toys to play with and they watch that box every night that seems to bring them such pleasure. Maybe I'm the one who is wrong. All I knew is fighting and distrust. Maybe I am the one who needs to change.'

Edwards smiled as he looked at Alice. Fierce Biter Queen or not, she was at her core still a young girl trying to figure out which was the right path to take.

'Alice, you don't need to change at all. I've seen the world torn apart once before when it looked like we had everything we needed to be happy. The point is that the more people have, the more they crave. That greed is what led us to ruin once before, and I'm afraid that Arun and the others never learnt that lesson.'

Alice asked the next question with a bit of hesitation, not wanting to seem totally ignorant.

'Doctor, this TV they watch so much—I don't see what's so interesting about watching some videos of people pretending to be what they aren't.'

Edwards laughed, his wrinkles creasing across his face.

'My dear, you have a way of perceiving things well beyond your age. The sad reality is that what they consider entertainment on TV is like a drug that dulls their ability to see the real world outside. The world where a bloody war still rages.'

Danish and Arjun entered the Looking Glass. Both looked quite agitated.

'Alice, we need to get to the Council building now. Arun's called a cabinet meeting and we need to be there as soon as we can.'

'What's going on?'

Arjun looked at Edwards.

'Doctor, it seems the Central Committee has sent a new message. They gave Arun a tablet, so he gets their postings directly, but we can see what they're saying here in the Looking Glass. Bring up their Intranet.'

When Edwards brought up the screen, they all read the announcement with a growing sense of dread.

The Central Committee had requested that the government of Wonderland cease all communications with the counter-revolutionaries in the American Deadland as such actions were detrimental to the creation of a peaceful people's revolution and would come in the way of further fraternal relations between the people of Wonderland and the Mainland.

Edwards whispered, 'Maybe they saw my posting.'

Arjun pretended to be throwing up, and Alice smiled.

'Arjun, it's the standard ridiculous propaganda they throw out.'

Danish just stood there, a grim expression on his face.

'Alice, I think Arun intends to do as they say.'

~* * * ~

'You cannot let them control the Looking Glass!'

Alice had never seen Danish this angry before. His cheeks had turned red and his breathing was jagged. Worried about the old man's health, Alice gently took his hand and asked him to sit down. As much as she shared Danish's sentiments, she knew that this was an argument they had little chance of winning. Over the months, the earlier flood of visitors to the Looking Glass had dried to a trickle. When the threat of imminent Red Guard attacks had reduced, people had almost inevitably started focusing on domestic squabbles and issues within Wonderland instead of worrying about a war that seemed distant. If anything, support for the Looking Glass would have gone down over the last few days. As Edwards had whispered to Alice, people would much rather watch inane soap operas than bother about the unpleasant realities of faraway wars.

Arun had himself spent a lot of time in the Looking Glass, and Alice knew that he was fond of Danish, so he was trying his best to placate the old man instead of forcing a decision.

'Danish, they do not want us to shut it down. We are still free to see the Intranet from the Mainland and we can continue to use our internal radio transmissions. All they ask is that we not have any contact with the Americans and that their technicians will come over to install some firewalls.'

Danish spat on the ground.

'Arun, listen to yourself! Today they are trying to control what we see; tomorrow they will try and control what we think. Soon we will become their puppets. They could not win this war through arms, but now they will conquer us with their cheap toys, clothes and cosmetics.'

The audience stirred.

Vince said, 'Arun, you know that the war rages in the American Deadland, a renewed struggle inspired by your own actions in creating Wonderland. I have lived in the Central Committee's labor camps and I can tell you that they see us as no more than pawns and slave labor. Every concession we make towards them makes us weaker in their eyes, and you know what they said about bullies, don't you? They feed on weakness.'

Arun sat down, his head in his hands.

'Folks, let's get real here. Do we want a renewed war? All I'm trying to do is to keep our people safe. How will posting messages to the Americans in any way help us make Wonderland safer? Tell me that and I'll listen to you.'

And so it was done. Two Red Guard technicians flew in, and undeterred by the murderous looks Danish gave them, installed software on the computers at the Looking Glass which would prevent them from accessing any of the pages uploaded from the American Deadland. Any second thoughts or concerns the people of Wonderland might have had were silenced by another plane-load of crates, filled with food, cosmetics, and another television.

They did not have to wait long for the next move in the intricate game of chess that Commissar Hu and his masters were playing. After the nightly soap opera, a grim faced woman appeared on TV, with a red 'breaking news' scroll across the screen.

'People of Wonderland, recent investigations have revealed a most shocking truth concerning the disturbances in the past in the area known as the Deadland. These have led to much misunderstanding between our nations. Newly discovered documents show that some Zeus officers in the Deadland had overstepped their authority and had engaged in illegal smuggling of people without any knowledge of the Central Committee. They were working hand in hand with smugglers in the Mainland who were running illegal farms and then selling food to the people in the

Mainland at exorbitant prices in a black market. Two of these smugglers have already accepted all charges against them and have been executed.'

There was a stunned silence among the hundreds gathered in front of the TV. Satish, who had dozed off, suddenly woke up. Arjun sensed what was coming and went to call Alice as the woman continued speaking.

'When their illegal activities were at risk of being discovered, they blamed the Central Committee and instigated the people of the Deadland against us. Then they engaged in terrorist attacks that started the unfortunate war between our nations. Now that our people are once more bound together by fraternal relations of love and respect, it's time we unmasked who these villains are. Ironically today these same men are in charge of Wonderland's security.'

Alice had now arrived, and she watched in shock as several photos appeared on the screen. There was Colonel Dewan, who had played a pivotal role in their struggle by believing in Alice and helping the resistance in the Deadland, until he paid the ultimate price by losing his life to the Red Guards. A string of officers followed—and finally there was Satish.

She saw several people in the crowd turn towards him. Satish was now on his feet, his eyes narrowed in anger.

'Those bastards!'

A meeting followed the next morning between Arun, Alice, Satish and Arjun.

'Arun, you do realize they are lying, don't you?'

For the first time in weeks, Arun looked actually scared. He had been in his element as Prime Minister, believing he was bringing peace to Wonderland and achieving a destiny he had thought had been taken from him forever. Now his place as little more than another pawn was becoming clearer and clearer to him.

'Satish, I sought refuge here with my family and

you saved us from Biters and Red Guards alike. I would trust you with my life any day. I was a politician before The Rising, so I know well what propaganda means and how it can be used and abused, but there's something I had never realized. Something that may yet prove to be our undoing.'

'What is that?' Alice asked.

'For people like me, Arjun, Satish, and others of our age, we knew what the world was like before The Rising. We know what messages are likely to be no more than propaganda and what we can really trust. We know that the Chinese were not exactly our allies and how their political system was so different from our democracy. But more than half the people in Wonderland were either born after The Rising or are too young to remember any of this. They take everything they see at face value; they are the ones most excited by the shiny toys and TV shows, and they are the ones the Central Committee is winning over with these messages.'

'They could not defeat us, so they steal our children's minds,' Arjun growled.

'Alice, we need to defuse and manage the situation. I will issue a statement that there must be a mistake and someone is trying to frame Satish.'

Alice stood. 'My father used to tell me something about why he never worked for the Central Committee despite being asked to, and why he always ensured our settlement remained independent in spite of all the difficulties we faced. He used to say that a leash, even if made of the finest silk, is still a leash.'

The meeting ended with Arun's departure. He planned to issue a statement immediately.

When he was gone, Satish looked at Alice. 'What are you going to do?'

'I think the time's coming when we'll be needed to fight once more. Spread the word among your men that they should make sure our heavy weapons are ready to use.'

Satish grinned.

'About time we did what we should have done long ago.'

As he turned to leave, Alice cautioned, 'Just don't do anything hasty. Lie low for now.'

She turned to see Arjun grinning broadly.

'What's so funny, Arjun?'

'I never cease to be amused by how you order around people three times your age, and how they listen to you.'

Later that day, Alice was called urgently to town. She raced there on her bike, hoping it was not another Biter attack. When she arrived, she found that it was almost as bad. Two of Satish's men had been eating at McDonald's when a couple of teenagers had made comments about Satish being a criminal. Words had been exchanged and before anyone could defuse things, a fight had broken out. One of the boys was in hospital with a broken nose and a large crowd had gathered in front of Arun's office, demanding that Satish's men either be disarmed or confined to barracks.

One woman shrieked, 'These men are too used to war. They don't know how to live in civilized company anymore.'

Alice glared at her and the woman shrunk under her gaze.

'You have what you call civilized company because soldiers like them bled for you. Don't forget that.'

Arun was inside with Arjun and Satish, who seemed livid.

'Arun, these boys are our best fighters. There is no way I will disarm them.'

Arun rubbed his forehead absently, trying to deal with a throbbing headache.

'This is all going crazy. Look, can you please put your recon teams in a barracks for a day or two till things cool down? Arjun, can your men handle security till then?'

Arjun shook his head sadly. 'My boys can break up fights and help drunks home, and of course they could shoot Biters when they were in the Deadland. But they are not trained combat soldiers like Satish's men, so if there's any trouble with the Red Guards, they won't last too long.'

'But there aren't any Red Guards around, are there?'

Alice said, 'Not yet, but I'm sure we will cross paths with them soon enough.'

~* * * ~

Back in Ladakh, Hu was seated in Chen's office, the chess set in front of him as usual, looking more complacent and smug than ever. As events had unfolded in Wonderland over the last few days, Chen had finally begun to grasp the true extent of what Hu and the Central Committee had planned.

'Comrade General, do you see now how this war is being waged and won? I don't care about those savages and their pathetic piece of land, but the fertile lands of Northern India are needed to feed our people, and we need labor to resume working on farms and in the camps back in the Mainland.'

Chen was silent, but Hu fixed him with an expectant look. Okay, if the Commissar wanted groveling and positive validation, Chen would oblige. If it helped him save the lives of hundreds more young conscripts from being thrown away in meaningless battles, he would play along.

'Comrade Commissar, the plan is certainly something I would never have thought of. It's reassuring that the Central Committee has been able to find a more peaceful solution to achieve our goals.'

Hu laughed.

'Comrade Commissar, did I say something to amuse you?'

Holding his belly, tears standing out in his eyes, Hu said, 'Who told you that there is to be no more bloodshed?' Opening his hand, he produced a chess piece. 'You see, Comrade, our game is a little bit different than a normal game of chess. In this game, the White King can be taken off the board and the game will continue.'

~* * * ~

Arun pulled his jacket around him, trying to keep out the chill. He remembered a time when he actually welcomed Delhi winters, enjoying hot cups of tea in the heated comfort of his bungalow. In the Deadland, winters had meant nothing but misery and huddling in old, tattered blankets. So it was no surprise that the latest shipment from the Central Committee had generated much excitement, as it had brought crates packed with soft woolen sweaters and blankets. Arun had stood proudly as people had openly cheered and clapped. That one moment had brought home to him that he had finally made progress in being a true leader to his people. Wonderland may have been forged in blood and war, but Arun would be the one who brought the beginnings of peace and prosperity to his people.

The flight had also brought with it a message for Arun from Commissar Hu. The Commissar wanted to meet Arun alone to discuss some important matters. Arun had been requested to not share this request with anyone else: the message had euphemistically stated, 'Do not share broadly until we have met to prevent counter-revolutionary elements in Wonderland from sabotaging our continuing partnership'. Arun knew that the 'elements' being referred to were Alice and Satish, and he was fine with that. He had sought refuge in Wonderland like thousands of others and watched Alice and her followers wage the war that had brought them some breathing space, but while Arun never doubted her courage or skill with weapons, he did not think she had the vision needed to realize that no society could exist in a perpetual state of war. The only way out was to bring about some semblance of stability and peace. Arun was well versed enough in the ways of politics to know that the Central Committee had not been sending all their shiny gifts out of the goodness of their hearts. They would want something back in return, and he guessed that was what this meeting was about. His best guess was that the Central Committee would want to restart the farms in the plains where labor from the Deadland had once worked. When he and the others in the Deadland had been scavenging to survive, many settlements had sent people to these farms to buy some degree of security from Biter hordes. At that time, Alice's vision of these being slave camps and her offering freedom seemed compelling. Now, with a more settled presence in Wonderland, Arun believed that it could be a more equal exchange. He could promise some share of the harvest from these farms in return for assured supplies of goods that would really set Wonderland on its path back to civilization. Already he had a mental list that included more generators, bicycles to help people get around more easily, and a large screen and projector to open the first movie theatre in Wonderland—something that had been much in demand once people had started getting used to the daily dose of TV soaps.

This was what national leaders did, wasn't it? Trade with other nations to bring prosperity to their people; create a vision for a peaceful, stable society; and end long, festering wars. So Arun had slipped away at night, riding a bicycle to the borders of Wonderland and then arriving at the agreed rendezvous point. Part of him was worried at being out in the Deadland alone at night, and he nervously fingered the pistol tucked into his belt, but the excitement of a major new agreement with the Central Committee overrode that nervousness.

Arun had been so lost in thought that he almost missed seeing the sleek black helicopter that had landed a hundred or so meters away. It had arrived without making any noise, and looked like the helicopter that Vince loved to play around with. A figure stepped out, barely more than a smudge in the darkness. From a distance, in the dull glow reflected from the cockpit of the helicopter, it looked like a Red Guard officer, with the trademark slanted cap. But as Arun got closer, he was surprised to see that the officer seemed to be a woman. He had never encountered a female Red Guard before and wondered if she was an aide who had come to fetch him to meet the Commissar.

A nervous knot formed in his stomach. He did not want to be taken anywhere alone by the Red Guards. Talk of fraternal relationships was great when he was in the relative safety of Wonderland, but not out here when he was all alone.

The Red Guard officer strode toward him.

He had a tactical radio strapped to his belt, and the frequency was set to the Looking Glass. He knew Danish would be there, and while the old man would hardly be able to offer much help, he could alert Alice and Satish. It was a sobering thought as he realized that when he was faced with imminent danger the two people he had done most to undermine in his attempt to gain power were the only two people he thought he could count on to help him.

The Red Guard officer was now mere feet away. In perfect English she said, 'Greetings, Mr. Prime Minister. It is an honor to meet you.'

Hearing her polite greeting reassured Arun and he

walked towards her, still unable to make out her features in the dark.

'Greetings, is Commissar Hu here, or do I need to go anywhere else to meet him?'

The officer chuckled. Then her voice changed, taking on a harder edge.

'Prime Minister, my brother died somewhere here in the Deadland, cut to pieces by the Yellow Witch and her monsters.'

Arun stopped in mid-stride.

'I listened to survivors of his unit talk about how people like you cheered and clapped as they were hunted down by her. It was a war, I admit that, but why would you allow the slaughter of those who were willing to surrender?'

After a moment of fumbling for a response, Arun said, 'No, such a thing never happened. We always let surrendered Red Guard units go. That was Alice's order.'

'You lie!'

Li spat out the words and took another step towards Arun. He saw her reach for something at her belt and, suddenly very scared, Arun took out the one signal flare he was carrying and lit it. As he held it in front of him, he got his first look at the Red Guard officer facing him. He took in the red, lifeless eyes, the teeth pulled back in a feral grimace, and the decaying, yellowed skin. He stumbled back, the flare falling to his feet.

'What are you?'

Li picked up the flare and held it close to her face.

'I am the Red Queen, dog!'

Arun clicked the transmit button on his radio. He screamed, 'Looking Glass, I need help!'

Before he could say another word, Li had crossed the distance between them in a single leap and hit him with an outstretched palm. Arun doubled over in pain as he felt his ribs crack. He struggled to his feet as Li pivoted, cracking the edge of her palm against Arun's nose. He felt warm blood spurt out over his face and mouth and he screamed in pain. He tried to reach for the gun at his belt, but Li grabbed his wrist in a lock, applying pressure until she heard the bones snap. Arun's screams became incoherent.

Li wanted to make him suffer more, but her orders were clear as to how this man was to die. She brought him close and then leaned forward, opening her mouth to bite. Behind her two of her Biters approached to finish the job.

~* * * ~

Danish had stepped out to stretch his legs. Sitting in front of the terminals and radio equipment for hours every day was not doing his aging joints any good. Not being able to access the American sites was frustrating but he had nowhere else to go, as he slept most nights in a small room adjoining the Looking Glass. He had decided to call it a night and sleep when he heard the scream on the radio. He rushed back inside, but he heard nothing else. Had he imagined it? He could have sworn he had just heard Arun scream. Falling down into his seat, he tried to call Arun's tactical radio.

'White King, do you copy? This is the Looking Glass.'

He flinched as he heard a low moan, sounding more like an animal in pain than a human being. That was followed by a roar that could have come only from a Biter.

EIGHT

'WHITE QUEEN, I think I saw some movement about a kilometer east of your current position.'

'Roger, White Knight. I'm on it.'

The moment they had been alerted by Danish to the transmission from Arun's radio, Alice, Satish and Arjun had been scouring the area around Wonderland. Arun's wife did not know where he had gone, other than the fact that he had stepped out late for a meeting. That set off alarm bells in Alice's mind, so they agreed to not only search Wonderland, but also the land bordering it. Vince was in his helicopter, using its motion sensors and heat detectors to aid in the search. Not knowing what they were getting into, Alice radioed Satish and Arjun to join her before they investigated what Vince had just spotted.

Vince reached the location well before they did and what he saw was clear. There was a heat signature in the darkness almost directly below him. From the limping way the figure seemed to be moving, it was either a badly wounded man or a Biter. He would have taken the helicopter down for a closer look but Alice had told him to stay in the air to provide warning in case this was a Red Guard trap.

Alice was riding her bicycle and so far had been

cautious in the darkness but was now pedaling as fast as she could. Arun and Satish were on their own bicycles just behind her. They had debated coming out in a jeep but Arjun had cautioned that it would make too much noise and alert any potential adversaries. From over Alice's head came the soft hum of the helicopter; she was close. Vince must have seen her on his sensors as he turned on the powerful spotlight below his copter, lighting up the figure below him.

It was Arun; Alice could recognize him from his clothes.

'Arun, are you okay?'

She dismounted from her bike and ran towards him, and then skidded to a stop when he raised his face to look at her. His right hand was clearly broken and hung limp at his side, his face was bloodied and torn, and he had several bite marks visible beneath his tattered and bloody shirt. His bald head was covered with blood and his red eyes had a vacant look in them. He looked at Alice and snarled and then took a step towards her, baring his teeth. Alice sensed Satish come to a crouch beside her, his rifle at his shoulder.

'Don't shoot,' she warned.

Alice had done this dozens of times with Biters that had joined her band, only she had never imagined doing this with someone who had been a person she had spoken with just hours ago. Removing the charred book from her belt, Alice held it above her head with her left hand.

'Stop and look at me!'

The way she had screamed her command startled even Arjun and Satish, who had never witnessed this ritual and took a step back. Arun bared his teeth and jumped at Alice, who sidestepped him and kicked him down with ease.

'You fool! Do you think I am a mere girl to be bitten? Look at me!'

Arun's eyes went to hers. He stopped.

'I am your Queen and this is the book that contains the prophecy that is our fate. As long as I hold it you will obey and follow me.'

Arun snarled again and was about to leap when Alice kicked him hard in the chest, sending him sprawling.

'Follow me or I will tear you to pieces. Look at me, look at the book and remember that you are destined to follow me.'

Arun stayed crouched, his voice a low growl, but he did not attack. Edwards had been curious about how Alice got the Biters to follow her, and she had told him her about her own experiences and also what she had witnessed among the Biters who had followed Dr. Protima. Edwards had said that perhaps it reflected the fact that even though they were now no longer fully human, Biters perhaps had one thing in common with people. Like people, Biters needed symbols to follow and believe in, and the charred copy of Alice in Wonderland had become such a symbol.

Alice knelt down and took a closer look at Arun. When Satish and Arjun joined her, he snarled at them but did not attack. Alice heard Satish draw in his breath.

'My God, who did this?'

Arjun replied, 'Probably one of those damn Biters the Red Guards seem to have following that Red Queen. Though why they would do this escapes me.'

Bunny Ears emerged from the darkness, looking first at the figure and then Alice.

'Bunny Ears, take him with you and teach him how to follow you. Keep him safe till we figure out what's going on.'

The bunny eared Biter grunted and then pulled Arun to his feet. As the trio watched him disappear into the darkness, Arjun said in a low voice, 'I may not have agreed with him, but he was not a bad man. He was just blinded by his ambition and the hate he had for Biters. Sometimes when we hate something too much, we are fated to become the very thing we hate.'

They took their time coming back into Wonderland as they swept the area where they had found Arun. Satish found indentations in the sand that could have been created by the landing gear of a helicopter but there was no way of being sure. They found some blood nearby, presumably Arun's, and a discarded signal flare. There was no doubt that Arun had come out here by himself to meet someone, but whom that had been was a mystery. Alice's mind went back to the so-called Red Queen she had encountered in battle and she found it easy to imagine her and her Biters setting an ambush for Arjun, though what the Central Committee would gain by doing this was uncertain.

Their first stop back in Wonderland was the Looking Glass, where Danish was waiting for them. When they told him what had happened to Arun, his eyes widened.

'I have a really bad feeling about this.'

Vince arrived at that moment. To Alice he said, 'So far the Reds have been playing us quite well. They've alienated you and Satish from the rest of Wonderland; they've made the humans and Biters stop working together; and they've got the youngsters in Wonderland eating out of their hands. Whatever they're trying to do with Arun has to be a part of that plan: gradually dividing people in Wonderland to weaken it.'

As if on cue, Danish spotted a new message flashing on the Central Committee Intranet. It was an invitation for the people of Wonderland to gather and watch a special news broadcast on TV that morning.

The word had spread like wildfire by the time of the broadcast, so thousands of people were gathered around the Council building, and Arjun had to bring the TV outdoors so more people could watch it. When even more people landed up, he ended up hooking up the second TV, too.

Several of those gathered asked where Arun was.

Arjun stepped up on a table. 'Folks, I have no idea what they want to broadcast, so please be silent so we can all hear.'

He made no mention of Arun. He, Alice, Satish, Vince and Danish had resolved not to let anyone else in on the secret of what Arun's fate had been until they got a better idea of what the Central Committee was up to.

Before long a red star replaced the static and then the familiar newscaster appeared. Today she looked even more somber than usual as she began her report.

'It is with profound regret that we must report the passing of one of our dear friends and a steadfast champion of the fraternal bonds between the Mainland and Wonderland.'

A buzz spread through the gathered crowd as she continued, 'Late last night, Arun Chowdhury, the Prime Minister of Wonderland, was apparently set upon by a group of wild Biters and killed. Please wait as we show photos from one of our circling drones.'

A series of photographs flashed across the screen. They were fuzzy and the night-vision optics gave them an eerie glow, but what they showed was clear enough. Arun lay sprawled across the ground with two Biters leaning over him.

Commissar Hu appeared on the screen next.

'I mourn the passing of a statesman who had the vision to see that our nations could put aside past misunderstandings and start a new relationship. It is clear that with the Zeus traitors having been exposed for the criminals they were and the so-called Queen losing control of her Biters, the people of Wonderland need security. If the Prime Minister, our dear brother, could not be protected, what will happen to ordinary citizens of Wonderland?'

Alice felt a stirring in the crowd and one or two

teenage boys pointed at her and Satish. But what Hu said next scared her more than any potential disturbance in the crowd.

'Dear brothers and sisters in Wonderland, we will not abandon you in this time of need. Until you are able to secure your own borders and elect a worthy successor to Comrade Arun, I am dispatching a small force to help secure your borders and protect you from these heinous Biter hordes.'

~* * * ~

'Dakotas at Netaji Subhas Chandra.'

It was the fifth time that day that the Americans had made that enigmatic transmission on the radio. While Danish had been unable to access the American websites, he had hidden Arun's old ham radio set when the Red Guard technicians had come, and had been using it to listen into what the Americans were saying. He had caught snippets about ongoing battles in the American Deadland and also repeated pleas for Wonderland to re-establish contact. Then had come the mysterious transmission, repeated several times every day for the last two days.

Vince asked, 'What the hell are they talking about?'

After the last TV transmission, Alice, Satish, Vince and Edwards had essentially sought refuge inside the Looking Glass. Satish's men were on edge, but he had asked them to stay in their barracks. Arjun was spending every minute passing through Wonderland, trying to soothe frayed tempers and nerves. A few young men had decided that attacking Satish would be a good idea, but Arjun had dissuaded them at the point of a gun. Wonderland was a powder keg about to explode at any minute, and Alice worried that when the Red Guards arrived they would be able to essentially take over Wonderland with little resistance.

'I have no idea how, but the Reds have made a

mistake and we need to use that against them.'

All eyes fell onto Arjun. He continued, 'They left Arun there, thinking he was dead. That Red Queen of theirs did not get transformed by being bitten. She and her Biters were created in a lab, so she probably has never seen a human get bitten and transformed. She did not know that a person looks dead and then wakes as a Biter after a few minutes. From their TV transmission, the Reds believe Arun is dead, maybe because they spotted Vince's helicopter and scooted before Arun woke up as a Biter.'

'Let's call everyone and tell them what's going on now! We must get organized and ready before any Red Guards get close,' Alice cried.

Satish shook his head. 'We will get ready, and we do need to tell people what happened to Arun, but we need to wait.'

'For what?'

'For us to be ready. I want all my recon teams back in the Deadland to act as a tripwire for Red Guards and to give us some warning, and I want my SAM teams deployed before we do anything that may get the Reds to act. But I can't do that now, not with the tensions in Wonderland. Let's wait till nightfall and get my men deployed. Then first thing tomorrow morning we can get Arun back here.'

Alice did not like the idea of waiting for one more night, but she saw reason in what Satish was saying. Armed troopers out in the streets now would likely only provoke confrontation. She also needed to get word to Bunny Ears, and that would take some time.

Suddenly Danish stood up, excitement shining in his eyes.

'I got it! I can't believe I never made the connection earlier!'

'What?'

Danish grabbed Alice by the shoulders, unable to stop himself from smiling.

'I figured out what the Americans have been trying to tell us. They would have seen Doctor Edwards' last post and I'm sure they're trying to get him out.'

Alice still had no idea what Danish was talking about.

'Netaji Subhash Chandra International Airport was the name given to the airport in Calcutta.'

Vince completed the thought for him. 'And Dakotas would refer to airplanes. Old DC-3s. It makes sense that without satellites for GPS or networks to run the navigation computers, the first planes flying are the old propeller driven ones like the Dakota. They must have made landings in Calcutta.'

Alice felt a surge of excitement. The Americans had found a way to reach what had once been the Indian subcontinent! They had found comfort in the radio broadcasts and web posts they had shared with the Americans since they told them that they were not waging a solitary war. Now there was a chance to make direct contact and, critically, to get Edwards to a location where he could help create a vaccine or a cure.

'Vince, you said you could get the helicopter to Calcutta, didn't you?'

'Yes, Alice. If I top up all the tanks and carry a bit of extra fuel, I could make it quite easily.'

'Then you must take the doctor and leave as soon as possible.'

Edwards stood up, shaking his head.

'Alice, an attack on Wonderland is imminent. We cannot abandon you at a time like this!'

Alice countered, 'That is precisely why you need to get away as fast as possible. I know that you need my blood sample and you are the only one who can help find a cure or a vaccine with it. We cannot risk you being here when the attack comes. Vince, take the doctor and get to Calcutta tonight.'

For a moment he seemed to weigh the decision.

Finally, he said, 'I'll do it.'

Then he was gone, riding his bike as fast as he could to get to the airport to prepare for the long flight.

To Arjun, Alice said, 'You need to make sure the doctor gets on the helicopter and leaves safely. Danish, tell the Americans that we are sending someone to Calcutta in a way that the Red Guards won't understand even if they intercept the transmission.'

Danish nodded. 'If only I could disable the bloody bugs those Red Guards placed in our computers I could have just messaged them.'

Next Alice looked at Satish. 'We need to get ready. The Red Guards may be here any time. I doubt they will launch an all out attack at first. They have been winning this war with deceit and stealth, and they will try to continue that. I expect them to start patrols outside Wonderland and then perhaps start dictating our policies and getting people to work on the old farms in return for their supposed security. I'll go and alert Bunny Ears and the others and get Arun ready; you get your men to prepare themselves.'

~* * * ~

Chen looked out of his window to see the black transport aircraft landing at the far end of the airstrip, well away from the prying eyes of the Red Guards at the base. Three of them had already disgorged their passengers and he had been told there was to be one more planeload. As soon as they landed, the passengers were met by Li on the tarmac and then herded into the far end of the base. Hundreds of Biters had been brought in for the coming operation and Chen felt a bit sick at the thought of what was to come. He had dedicated his life to the Central Committee under the illusion that the war against the Biters was necessary to protect what was left of human civilization. It was truly a perversity that the same Central Committee was now freely using Biters created in its labs to serve its purpose. However, all these thoughts were buried in Chen's mind, as Commissar Hu was standing right behind him, having flown in the previous night to personally oversee the operation—and while it had never been said aloud, to ensure that Chen stuck to the plan.

'Comrade General, are your men ready?'

Chen stiffened, weighing in his mind how he should reply, since the question was about the readiness not just of his men, but himself.

'Yes, Comrade Commissar, we are ready, though I must confess some of the men have been grumbling about policing duties in the Deadland when they had thought that phase of the war had long ended.'

Hu chuckled. 'Your men should learn to play chess, Comrade. That war never came to an end. We were just waiting for the right time to make our move. If my calculations are correct, the puppet government of this so-called Wonderland is now leaderless and their people are divided. Many of their youth, fed on our food and clothed in our finest fabrics, will see security in embracing us, and once more join our fold. Then, Comrade General, these savages will do as they were meant to: serve us in the farms in the plains. Food will once again flow to the Mainland, and our people will enjoy the prosperity of the people's revolution. We will win this war with little or no bloodshed, Comrade.'

Chen said nothing, but he knew that only politicians and fools believed that any war could be won without bloodshed.

~* * * ~

Alice watched the helicopter take off and fly eastwards. She hoped Vince and Edwards would get to their destination safely, but for now her concerns were more immediate. Satish had been getting in touch with his men, telling them to be ready. In the darkness of night, six missile teams armed with surface to air missiles and RPG launchers had moved to the outskirts of Wonderland. Arjun had also begun mobilizing his men. He knew that many of them had mixed feelings about Alice and Satish after the Biter attacks and the Red propaganda, so he told them that he wanted them to be on guard against any unrest caused by the power vacuum left by Arun's death. Despite the late hour, he had many of his men start neighborhood patrols, which ensured that if there was any trouble he would have a ready reserve of armed men to back up Satish's teams.

Alice felt a familiar buzz that she always seemed to feel at the prospect of upcoming battle. She had been told she had a keen edge when it came to combat, partly driven by years of training and living in the Deadland, and partly perhaps by her nature. Dr Protima had told her that part of the infection that turned humans into Biters activated the most primitive parts of their brain, making them hyper-aggressive. At times Alice wondered how true that was for someone who was only part Biter like her. Though she had kept it to herself, since her transformation it took a conscious effort to think strategically instead of impulsively in battle. That was what she was trying to focus on now.

'Alice, we cannot really do much if half of Wonderland thinks we are the enemy. What do you want to do about that?'

Alice turned to face Arjun.

'I am on my way now. You need to call a Council meeting and ensure as many people as possible join.'

There were still a couple of hours to go until sunrise and Alice pedaled her bike furiously as she crossed over to the Deadland. She passed one of Satish's recon teams hidden behind some bushes. She waved to them as she passed and while she did not hear them, the men whispered to themselves that when the Queen was up and about, battle would not be far behind.

She soon saw that danger was much more imminent than she had imagined. The light of a fire burned in the distance, and Alice ducked behind cover.

Poor stupid kids, she thought, wondering just how green these conscripts must be to light up a fire which would be visible for miles around. The thought that they were probably only a few years older than her never crossed her mind. She looked through the scope of her rifle and through the greenish glow of the night vision optics she saw six Red Guards huddled around the fire. Part of her felt sorry for them, but then in choosing to obey their orders they had sealed their fate. In her young life, if there was one thing she had learnt it was the fact that there was always a choice when it came to accepting tyranny. The cost of saying no might come with hardships and sacrifice, but it was never acceptable to say that there was no choice.

She would have preferred to bypass the six Red Guards, but they were directly in her path. Alice thought she could handle the six of them if she had the element of surprise, but there was no way of knowing how many other such teams had been inserted in the night in the name of providing security to Wonderland. Alice allowed herself a grin as she remembered what her father had once told her: that no matter how hard he tried subtlety was never going to be something he could teach her.

Removing a flash bang grenade from her belt, Alice began her slow approach. They were now barely twenty meters away and in the darkness did not spot her coming. If anything, sitting so close to the bright flame and staring at it had ruined their night vision. It was this that Alice would use to her advantage.

Alice pulled the pin on her grenade and threw it in a looping arc towards the men. The grenade landed just feet away from them and exploded in a dull thump, momentarily flashing more brightly than the fire.

The first two died without knowing who had shot them as carefully aimed single shots took them in the head or throat. Another Red Guard fired a wild burst from his rifle but fell as another round hit him. The remaining three men were now firing blindly, trying to pin down their attackers while they got their bearings. Alice was firing on the run, and dropped one more. Then she was amongst the two remaining men. The first fell like a chopped tree when Alice smashed his jaw in with the butt of her rifle. The last man was now screaming in terror when Alice pivoted on one foot and kicked him, sending him down. Without waiting to see if there were other Red Guards in the area that would inevitably come to the scene after seeing and hearing the gunshots, Alice ran straight towards the nearest Biter tunnel entrance, removing the branches arranged against the old drainage pipe and diving in.

It was as if she had entered another world altogether. It had been months since Alice had been inside the tunnels, but whenever she entered one, she could never forget the day this had all begun. The day she had dived into a tunnel after a Biter wearing strange bunny ears; the day she had discovered a strange subterranean world where the Biters lived with their mysterious Queen; the day when Alice discovered that her path in life was to take her very far from her settlement in the Deadland.

It was dark inside the tunnel and she lit a signal flare, holding it in her right hand. With her left hand she took out the book and held it before her. She didn't have to wait long. Within minutes of walking, a Biter appeared before her. She had been an old woman as a human, attacked and transformed in a hospital;

even now she had the needle of an IV drip attached to her right arm. Her face was relatively unscathed other than a terrible bite mark to the neck, and when she saw Alice she screamed and opened her mouth to bite. Alice held the book in front of her face and screamed, 'NO! I am the Queen and you will follow me!'

The Biter retreated, bowing her head down. Alice proceeded down the tunnel. She could now hear scurrying noises all around her in the tunnels. The word would have spread that the Queen was among the Biters. After a few more minutes of walking, she saw Bunny Ears sitting in a corner. Arun was beside him, absently chewing on his fingers. Alice would have loved to be able to tell Bunny Ears to show up with Arun where and when she wanted instead of having to take them with her, but she knew such level of thinking was beyond Biters. Then again, Biters did exactly as she wanted them to. They did not debate, they did not strategize, and they did not have personal political agendas. All things considered, there certainly were times when Alice enjoyed leading Biters more than humans.

Wonderland woke up to find itself ringed by Red Guard patrols. More than once, helicopters flew close to the city and then turned back.

'Should I just have one of them shot down to make a point?'

Arjun sniggered at Satish's suggestion. 'I don't doubt that time will come, but let's wait till we deal with our young rebels.'

More than a hundred young boys had gathered in front of the Cabinet. One of them, wearing clothes fresh from a Red Guard shipment, stepped forward.

'Arjun, why are you stopping us from joining the Red Guards?'

That morning another transmission had come in announcing an incoming message from the Central Committee. Commissar Hu had informed the people of

Wonderland that the heroic Red Guards had stepped in, braving the harsh Deadland and wild Biters to provide security to their brethren in Wonderland. He had asked for a hundred volunteers to come out of Wonderland help in the patrols.

Arjun answered, 'We do not take orders from the Central Committee and certainly we do not send our boys to work for them again. Obedience to tyrants is a habit that is hard to break once formed. Today in the name of security they ask for so-called volunteers. Tomorrow once again they will start taking our people to work on their farms or labor camps.'

Jeers went up from some members of the crowd.

The young man persisted. 'Don't you get it? Those bloody Biters have run amuck again and Arun's dead. The Central Committee has done nothing but help us.'

Arjun stepped forward, bringing his face to within inches of the young man, who took a nervous step back.

'They have done nothing to help us. They seek to buy our dependence and obedience—to conquer with their cheap clothes and shampoos what they could not with their armies. They want to make us sell our freedom by making us live in fear once more.'

Another boy shouted above the crowd, 'What other option do we have? To trust our safety to criminals and smugglers?'

Suddenly, the crowd began surging forward and Satish and Arjun began backing up towards the building. There were thousands of others who had gathered to hear the morning transmission and most of them stood as mute onlookers. Yet it took only a few to start a mob.

Satish tried reasoning with the boys. 'Look, we have all fought together and lived together like a family. We need to work together, not fight each other.'

A fist shot out and grazed Satish on the chin. He calmly grabbed the wrist and snapped it, hearing bones crack. Another boy grabbed him by the hair but he kicked the feet out from under the boy. Arjun had his finger on the trigger of his gun, but he knew that if he fired there would be a bloodbath, and that was just the kind of chaos that the Red Guards wanted to take advantage of.

Two more boys tried to grab Satish and he lost his footing in the surge of the mob. Arjun had his rifle out now and was about to fire in the air, but before he could, a series of shots rang out. Everyone stopped and looked to see Alice standing there, rifle in hand. Just behind her stood Bunny Ears and a second Biter. When people saw his clothes and his bloodied face, there were gasps of horror and surprise.

'Arun,' someone whispered.

Alice walked towards the mob surrounding Satish and they melted before her. She climbed the stairs leading into the building and said in a loud, commanding voice, 'I'm glad at least you remember how to get angry and to fight. I had thought the people of Wonderland had forgotten how to be angry about all that had been taken from us by the Central Committee. But if you have to be angry, if you have to fight, do it against the real enemy, not amongst ourselves.'

There was a stunned silence as Arun stepped forward and the deception of the Central Committee became clear. Arjun told everyone about the Biters the Red Guards had unleashed and how they had divided the people of Wonderland.

Alice looked at the gathered crowd. 'I don't have time to convince each and every one of you. The Red Guards are right outside our borders and we will soon be surrounded. Who is with me?'

When Arjun and Satish stood beside her, Bunny Ears shuffled along to join them. At first only a few of those in the crowd moved—but then more and more hands lifted in the air, more and more cries of support rose up.

Smiling, Alice walked away.

'Get ready. Wonderland just declared war on the Red Guards.'

NINE

'THE HEROIC RED Guards have fanned out across the Deadland to ensure that our brethren in Wonderland can sleep secure in the knowledge that in this time of need they are not alone.'

Someone spat on the ground, another shouted abuse, and Arjun began to see a perceptible change in the mood of the gathered crowd. Many of the younger folks still seemed skeptical, but Arun's reappearance as a Biter had given many of them reason to doubt what the Central Committee had been telling them. Now seeing the news footage being streamed on the TV showing aerial footage of Red Guard units being air-dropped across the Deadland was a sobering dose of reality. A few of them still shouted out that perhaps the Red Guards meant no imminent harm, but then the ominous announcement was repeated.

'We repeat our request to the people of Wonderland. Our intelligence indicates that hordes of Biters are about to attack. Please let Red Guards inside the city center to help secure your homes and families and please cooperate with them.'

It was the smartest invasion Arjun had ever seen. To take away people's liberty in the name of providing them security, to take away freedom in the name of fighting terror, was not a new tactic. But the Central

Committee had pulled off a nearly flawless plan, the one weak link being the fact that they had not bargained for Arun having survived the attack. They still did not know Arun's fate and that element of surprise was something Arjun and the others hoped to capitalize on. Alice and Satish had already left to start coordinating the defenses, but Arjun's job was to ensure that they could prepare for the house to house fighting that would be inevitable if the Red Guards got inside the city limits. He did not harbor any delusions that everyone would believe that the Central Committee had played them all as a prelude to an invasion, but he got the feeling that he had managed to convince enough of a critical mass. More importantly, it looked like at least the threat of open civil war that had been plaguing Wonderland was finally something that was no longer hanging over all their heads.

~* * * ~

Chen saw three more helicopters take off, laden with conscripts straight from the Mainland. Hundreds of Red Guards had been sent out overnight on their supposed aid mission. That was what they had been told in their camps in Shanghai and Beijing and he had not done anything to contradict that. He knew he could not do that with Hu looking over his shoulder, but he also knew that in not saying anything to these young men he had essentially condemned many of them to a near certain death. He felt the sting of tears and tried to blink them away. He had almost thrown away his career and his life by surrendering a base instead of having all the men there massacred, but now he had done nothing to stop the bloodshed that was about to follow. Sure, he could rationalize that his dissent would count for little, since he would likely be arrested and sent off to the Mainland, or perhaps even just be executed on the spot for treason given his previous stint at a labor camp. But rationalizing never compensated for not doing the right thing.

Hu was right next to him, smiling.

'See, Comrade General. Our plan is working like clockwork. We will get what we want without much bloodshed.'

Weighing his words carefully, Chen said, 'Comrade Commissar, from my experience this Alice and her friends will not go down without a fight.'

Hu chuckled. 'One mongrel girl and a handful of former mercenaries are all that is left of her army. How long will they last without popular support in Wonderland? If anything, once the next phase begins our boys will be welcomed as liberators.'

Li was looking at a photograph of her family. This was the last photograph that she retained of her entire family together- before her mother had fallen in The Rising, and her father and brother been shipped off to the Deadland. She wished she could cry, that she could shed a tear for what had been taken from her by the savages in the Deadland, but she had come to realize that tears were not for her anymore. Now all that mattered was carrying out her mission and avenging the deaths of her father and brother by shattering the terrorist regime of this so-called Wonderland. She had been keenly following the news reports and she knew that the people of Wonderland had cast away the yellow haired witch and her men. With her latest mission, Li would help bring the common people of Wonderland into the fold of the Central Committee, and then she would have a free hand in hunting down and killing the witch and her followers. She remembered her last encounter with the witch and reminded herself that she would not make the mistake of underestimating her again. Before Li had lashed out in haste in her quest for vengeance. This time she would operate with more deliberation and caution.

To the Biters kneeling before her, she shouted, 'Come on, glory awaits us.'

~* * * ~

Danish was sitting in the Looking Glass, going through all the Central Committee transmissions. With all that had happened in the previous few days, he had begun to see patterns in what their propaganda meant for actions on the ground. In the last hour, the talk had shifted to one of reported imminent Biter threats to Wonderland and how the hapless and leaderless citizens were at the mercy of this new terror. He knew it was largely aimed at the masses back in the Mainland, preparing them for inevitable casualties, but it also told him the nature of the attack that was to unfold. Satish had argued that they should focus on the anti-air and RPG teams since the edge the Red Guards would have lay in their air support and their armored vehicles. Danish was no military strategist but months of studying the Central Committee broadcasts had given him some insight into how their minds worked. He knew that popular support for any military action in the Deadland was wafer thin and there had been growing unrest in Mainland cities. So any outright invasion was going to be a very risky move. Yet the Central Committee badly needed the farms in the plains and labor to work them, otherwise the discontent caused by food shortages and by having to work long hours in farms was going to push the masses in the Mainland over the edge. The Central Committee needed to control the Deadland again, but the political cost of a full-scale invasion was going to be prohibitive.

Given those constraints, Danish had to grudgingly admire the plan the Central Committee had put in place. If Arun had not been found the way he was, it was very likely that, at this very moment, Wonderland would have been on the verge of civil war. Then the Red Guards could have just stepped in, welcomed into the people's arms. If Danish's reading were correct, the Central Committee would not ideally want the bloodshed associated with a frontal assault. They still seemed to think that Arun was dead and that the people of Wonderland had marginalized Alice and Satish. All the talk of impending Biter attacks could mean only one thing.

~* * * ~

Alice was lying down on the ground, hidden behind some bushes. There were two of Satish's men just behind her. They had ventured out more than two kilometers from the borders of Wonderland to cut off the Biter attacks that were likely on the way. There was really no way to anticipate exactly where the attacks would come from, but one thing was certain: the Biters and their Red Queen would have to be travelling together. There was no way Red Guards would be transporting a helicopter full of Biters into battle without her around to control them. That meant that there would have to be only one landing spot. Three deep recon teams had gone further ahead to warn of incoming helicopters. The Deadland around them was crawling with Red Guards and Alice and her group had already eliminated a squad of Red Guards who had stumbled upon them. Satish was with another team a kilometer to the west.

Alice's radio buzzed to life.

It was from a recon team to the east. 'White Queen, I think I see birds in the sky.'

Just then, another team called in approaching helicopters to the west.

She called Satish. 'White Rook, the birds to the west are yours. I'll watch the ones coming my way.'

She nodded to the two men with her, one of who was carrying an RPG launcher. She had considered bringing along teams equipped with SAMs, but carrying the heavy surface to air missiles would have meant losing much of the stealth they needed to get around the Red Guards teeming around them. She felt a keen sense of anticipation at the prospect of meeting the Red Queen again. She knew that the only possible outcome when the two of them met was a fight to the death, but at the same time she felt curious about whom this girl had been. What had made her hate Alice and the people of Wonderland so much? Alice closed her eyes and remembered the young Chinese girl, virtually a mirror image of her. As far as Alice knew, this Red Queen was the only other person in the entire world like her. In a different life, Alice might have liked to have the chance to sit and talk to her, to understand how she was coping with all the dilemmas and heartbreaks that came with being a young girl who could never be fully human again. Unfortunately, the only thing that they could share in this life was the moment when one of them died at the other's hand.

She heard the approaching helicopter before she saw it. She noted with some disappointment that it was not one of the black stealthy helicopters that seemed to carry the Red Queen.

The battle for Wonderland was about to begin.

~* * * ~

'The latest news is that terrorist forces are attacking Red Guard units in the Deadland. Intelligence indicates that terrorist factions led by disgraced Zeus mercenaries and the self-proclaimed Queen of Wonderland are trying to take advantage of the power vacuum in Wonderland. Our Red Guards are rushing to the aid of our brethren in Wonderland in fighting back these terrorists.'

The statement posted on the Central Committee Intranet was clear enough. Fighting had begun. Chen closed his eyes, thinking of the young conscripts whom he had sent to their deaths. Most of them were little more than scared boys rustled up from the Mainland with minimal military training, fed on a diet of horror stories about Biters and the terrible savage humans who lived in the Deadland. They had known no better than to trust a senior officer like Chen, and he had failed them all by sending them into the meat grinder that the campaign to win over the Deadland had become.

It was a truism in most wars that young soldiers paid with their lives to uphold the lies told by old politicians, but that did not make it any easier for Chen. He saw Hu at the control center, gloating in what he thought was to be his moment of triumph.

'Comrade General, the Supreme Leader of the Central Committee has been expressing a desire to retire and dedicate the rest of his life to serving the people. If I succeed in the conquest of Wonderland, I may be offered the job, and I will reward your loyalty handsomely. How would you like to be Commissar in my place?'

Chen's smile was enough for Hu, and he returned to monitoring broadcasts. Chen found himself imagining what it would feel like to take his gun and put a bullet in Hu's head. It would take no more than a couple of seconds to end this madness. With immense willpower, he was able to control himself. But in that fleeting moment, something changed within Chen. He knew that the next time he was ordered by men like Hu to send boys to their deaths, he would not be able to go through with it.

Alice watched the smoke trail of the rocket snake out from her right, heading towards the helicopter that had just landed a couple of hundred meters away. Another recon group had already encountered a Red

Guard landing and was engaged in a vicious firefight. Part of Alice wanted to wait for the occupants of the helicopter to disembark so that she could see whether the Red Queen was one of them, but she didn't want to lose any of the advantage of surprise she had. The rocket hit the cockpit, enveloping the front of the helicopter in a bloom of smoke and dust. The pilots were killed outright and several injured, bleeding Red Guards stumbled out of the passenger compartment. A few of the uninjured Red Guards had their weapons ready, searching for an enemy they could not see. Alice centered her scope on an officer who seemed to be in charge and was trying to rally his men. This was not the helicopter that would bring the Red Queen and her Biters, but the fate of the men who had just landed in it had already been sealed. Alice exhaled slightly and pulled the trigger.

~* * * ~

Arjun was dealing with chaos of a sort he had never handled before. He had spent years living in the Ruins, leading his motley crew of 'Ruin Rats' in running battles against Biters and the occasional Zeus patrol. So fighting in built up urban areas was nothing new for him or for many of the others who had joined him in their months of warfare against the Red Guards. Now, however, there was a subtle but important difference. People were no longer preparing to hide and fight in ruins that belonged to nobody other than perhaps the ghosts of their previous owners. Now they were preparing to fight for buildings they had come to consider home. All morning the TV had been carrying news reports of battles between the Red Guards and 'terrorists' and intelligence reports of impending Biter attacks. Regardless of where their trust lay, every single person in Wonderland knew a few things for certain now. The Central Committee was lying. Arun was not dead. Alice and her supporters were not trying to take over power by force. And finally, whatever the Central Committee said, people were not sure they wanted the Red Guards so close to their homes.

The positive side was that it had galvanized everyone into action. The negative was that as the old saying went, every man's home was his castle, and now every man was trying to be his own commander. Arjun knew that they would not survive long if they fought as small, isolated units, and he began to realize just how badly the months of peace had hurt their preparedness. A society at peace can be a wonderful one, but only if it never forgets how to wage war if needed.

Arjun and his men were trying to rally people into fire teams and create natural choke points among the buildings where they could trap incoming forces. The boys who had attacked him and Satish were now standing nearby, looking slightly sheepish. Arjun walked up to them. 'What's the matter?'

One of them answered, 'We all came into Wonderland with our families a few months ago. We don't know much about the tactics and tricks your men talk about. Tell us what we can do.'

Arjun sized him up. 'How many of you have killed a man or a Biter?'

Every single one of them raised his hand. Nobody could have grown into adolescence in the Deadland without knowing how to take a life.

'Then you all know most of what you need to know. I'll keep the older folks inside the city, but you are young and fast. I need you to do something that you don't need much tactics for.'

The boy looked perplexed.

'What do we need to do?'

Arjun smiled. 'You need to run as fast as you can.'

~* * * ~

'White Rook, this is Looking Glass. Do you have a parking space ready for our cars?'

Satish heard Danish and answered in the negative. From being their window to the outside world, Danish and his Looking Glass had now effectively become their command and control center. With his access to the Red Guard Intranet and transmissions, he could provide some forewarning of what may come their way. He also had the main radio switchboard, and so was vital for team-to-team coordination. Danish had been asking where to send their only real heavy land weapons: the three jeeps that had been fitted with rocket launchers captured from downed Red Guard helicopters. Without a clear idea of where the assault would come from, Satish did not want to risk exposing the jeeps to air strikes, so they had been kept well hidden.

His group of six had already had a skirmish with a group of Red Guards, leaving three Red Guards and one of his men dead. Now he was waiting for the helicopter that was supposedly flying towards their position.

One of his men whispered to him, 'Sir, I see it. There!'

He followed the man's outstretched hand and saw a black speck appear in the morning sky. Satish's team had been closer to Wonderland's borders than Alice, so he had a SAM unit nearby and he radioed for them to come in. Within a minute, two men jogged by, one of them carrying the large tube shaped missile launcher.

'Sir, I see three choppers.'

Satish began to reconsider his options. If there had been only one helicopter, he would have ordered it shot down without a second thought, but with three incoming choppers that would be a risky proposition.

Even if they managed to shoot one down with the first shot, the others would be onto them before they managed to reload. He had mere seconds in which to decide, and he barked to his men, 'Everyone, take cover! We'll get them when they land.'

Now the helicopters were close enough that Satish could see details. One was a black helicopter of the sort Vince had flown out to Calcutta; another was a larger and noisier transport helicopter; and the third was a smaller, sleek gunship. So far every indication had been that the Red Queen and her Biters flew in on the stealthy helicopter, but he had no way of knowing which of the choppers she'd be in now.

The two transport helicopters came down to land about five hundred meters away from Satish's position, but the gunship remained in the air. Satish knew the Biters inside the transport helicopter were the primary threat but if he attacked them first, he would be vulnerable to attack from the air. Making a split second decision, he ordered his men to fire their SAM at the gunship and ordered his man armed with the RPG launcher to fire at the black helicopter.

The missile snaked up towards the helicopter, and while the Red Guard pilot saw it and tried to evade, at such close range he really did not have a chance. The gunship exploded from a direct hit and its wreckage came falling down like a rainstorm of fire and metal.

On seeing the gunship fall, Red Guards began to troop out of the black helicopter. Satish screamed at his men to stop, to redirect to the other helicopter, which would hold the Red Queen and her Biters—but he was too late. The RPG hit the helicopter near the door, obliterating the Red Guards who were still trying to jump out. The few who had made it outside took cover and began firing at Satish and his men.

In the distance, he saw a female form in a Red Guard uniform run towards Wonderland, followed by dozens of Biters.

He had failed. The Red Queen had entered Wonderland.

~* * * ~

'People of Wonderland, this is an urgent message for you. Stay in your houses and do not try and interfere with the ongoing security operation against the intruding Biter hordes. Red Guards are coming to your assistance.'

Danish sat upright as the message flashed on his screen. A second later, he got a report on the radio that the same message was being repeated on the TV news broadcasts. That could mean only one thing: that Alice and Satish's teams had somehow failed and hostile Biters were approaching Wonderland. Now it would be up to Arjun to stop them and the Red Guards before things got totally out of control. Alice had briefed him on what to do in a situation like this and he patched her in on the radio so that she could communicate directly with the frequency the Red Guard Commissar had been using for his broadcasts lately.

Chen was sitting at the control center, thinking of the conscripts running into an urban battleground for which they were neither prepared nor trained. Many of the poor fools actually thought that they were going to receive a hero's welcome.

The radio operator took off his headset and beckoned to Chen.

'Comrade General, we have an incoming transmission from Wonderland.'

Chen put on the headset.

'This is General Chen of the Red Guards. Who am I speaking with?'

The answer sent a shiver down his spine. It was a voice that had haunted him since he had looked into the yellowed eyes of a young girl who had become Queen.

'General, you should remember me. My name is Alice Gladwell.'

Hu had come up behind him and asked Chen to put the broadcast on the speaker.

'This is Commissar Hu. I want to speak to some legitimate representative of the elected government of Wonderland, not an upstart terrorist and counter-revolutionary.'

There came a laugh from the other end. 'Commissar Hu, it is rich of you to talk of democracy and elections. I have no time for small talk. Tell your men to stay away from Wonderland while we destroy this Red Queen and her Biters.'

'The people of Wonderland –'

Alice cut him off. 'They know what you have been plotting. Arun is not dead. He became a Biter and is now with us. Now call off the Red Guards or I will be forced to kill them all.'

With that Alice ended the call. Chen looked at Hu, feeling numb with fear for what was to befall his men.

'Comrade Commissar, the plan is failing. If they truly know the truth then they will not be divided; elements among them will not welcome our boys. It will be a death trap for them.'

Pulling Chen aside, Hu addressed him in a harsh growl. 'Your critics in the Central Committee were right. You had lost your courage in the Deadland, and deserved to die in a labor camp. I resurrected your career because I needed your experience, but now I see that you have no nerve left for battle after all. That witch is just bluffing.'

The men in the control center looked at the two officers with wide eyes. For a moment Chen just stood in shock; then he straightened.

'Comrade Commissar, you plot in offices, pretending the world is a chessboard and people pawns to be moved from one square to another. I have news for you, Comrade. In the real world, those pawns bleed and die, and one day that river of blood will drown you and the other old monsters in the Central Committee.'

Hu looked like he had been slapped and then recovered. He motioned to the four black-clad bodyguards he had bought with him from the Mainland.

'Comrade General Chen seems to be suffering from fatigue brought on by his tireless efforts in driving forth the people's revolution. I think he needs some rest to recover his revolutionary fervor. Kindly escort him to his quarters.'

Chen reached for the gun at his belt, but strong hands grabbed him, and he was pulled away outside the room.

Hu looked around at the terrified looking Red Guards in the room.

'Comrades, does anyone else have any doubts about the war we are waging against counter-revolutionaries and terrorists that I can help dispel?'

Every single man looked down, unwilling to meet his gaze.

'Very well. Now, let us see how long this witch lasts against our own Red Queen.'

~* * * ~

Neel watched the first Biters come into view from his second floor window. He was more terrified than he had ever been, and he wondered if the two boys with him were as scared as he was. Still, at sixteen he was the oldest of the three and he could not appear weak in front of the others. He had volunteered for sentry duty when Arjun had asked for volunteers and his job was to watch for Biters who were supposed to be entering Wonderland. He had a pistol in his hand, and while his father had taught him how to shoot, he had not touched the gun in the last year that they had been living in Wonderland. He now saw six or seven Biters almost directly below him and he knew that shooting at them would achieve little. There was no way he could kill all of them. He needed to get word to Arjun or one of the other adults nearby.

Suddenly the boy next to him keeled over, blood spurting from a wound to the neck. The second boy screamed in terror, only to be silenced by another bullet to the head. Neel crouched low, too scared to move. Biters could never shoot like that. Then again, he had no idea that Li was just behind the Biters, taking out targets with her rifle, clearing the path. Red Guards were going to be just behind.

Hu's plan was to let the Biters cause some mayhem before the Red Guards got to the city center and placed Wonderland under 'protective custody' until they could have an election where someone sympathetic to the Central Committee could be installed as a puppet. With everything that had happened, he hoped that enough people in Wonderland would see that allying with the Central Committee was the only way to get security. As for Alice and her followers, Hu had more than enough Red Guards headed for the Deadland to deal with them. So far his plan had gone almost exactly as he had thought it would unfold.

Arjun watched the first Biter appear on the scope of his rifle. There were four; a good number. Just as they passed a building, Arjun pressed down on a nearby plunger, detonating the improvised explosive device inside the construction. The explosion tore off much of the side of the building and obliterated the Biters.

There was no way to guard all of Wonderland's many routes, so Arjun and Satish had decided to essentially focus on defending the city center. His scouts were in the outskirts in constant radio contact with the Looking Glass, and Danish had managed to piece together a pretty comprehensive picture of the battle as it unfolded. There seemed to be about fifty or so Biters who had entered Wonderland, and other than a group of six spotted traveling as a group with the Red Queen, the others were marauding at will. That made them relatively easy targets to pick off, but it also meant that many different teams were engaged in hunting them down, leaving precious few defenders to guard against the Red Guards who were almost certainly now entering Wonderland.

Captain Tso was leading his squad of eight Red Guards into the ruins. They had been helidropped just two kilometers away and from what he had already made out from the radio reports of other helicopters being shot down, they had been lucky to not be ambushed as they landed. He motioned for his men to stop as he scanned the buildings in front of him. His men had no combat experience but Tso had spent two tours of duty in the Deadland and hated having to go into such a congested area where an enemy sniper could be hiding in every window. But his orders had been clear. They were to go into the city and ensure safe passage for the armored carriers that were to soon follow, carrying more Red Guards. He had discounted much of the propaganda that the Commissar had spouted about them going into the city to save the hapless citizens from Biters. He had spent enough time in the Deadland to know that the people there had no love lost for Red Guards, especially since the Yellow Witch had taken over command. But orders were orders, and he just hoped that he did not lose too many of the boys walking behind him.

One of them shouted, 'Comrade Captain, I see a young boy sitting there. Maybe he needs our help.'

Tso looked to see a boy of no more than ten sitting calmly by the roadside, watching them. Three of Tso's men jogged over. Something did not look right to Tso and he raised his riflescope to his eyes to take a closer look. He saw the boy's hand close around something and before he could shout a warning to his men running towards the boy, a bomb exploded near them.

When the smoke cleared, all three Red Guards were down and the boy was nowhere to be seen.

~* * * ~

Alice was pedaling as fast as she could, towards the last location where the Red Queen had been sighted. Arjun's teams had neutralized many of the Biters and small groups of fighters were stopping advance elements of Red Guards with snipers and improvised explosive devices, but not yet the Red Queen, who was now pushing deeper into the city. Satish had also ordered most of his men to fall back, other than a few teams he was leading left on the borders with RPGs to ambush incoming APCs. It now looked like the fate of Wonderland would hang in house-to-house fighting.

Alice spotted movement to her right and came to a skidding halt as she saw three or four Biters. She unslung her rifle and fired, bringing two down with headshots. She was about to fire again when she saw a familiar figure emerging from behind a Biter.

Alice was once again face to face with the Red Queen.

TEN

L I STOPPED WHEN she saw Alice and for a second the two girls just stood there, looking at each other. Then Li motioned to the two Biters remaining with her to attack, and they started towards Alice. Li knew that they would never stand a chance, but they'd buy her time.

Alice calmly dispatched both Biters with a single shot to the head, but that had given Li the time to get off a shot of her own. Alice tried to roll aside, but the bullet grazed her neck as she came up in a crouch and raised her own rifle. Li had learnt the lessons of the last battle, and this time she would take her time to destroy the witch and not act in haste.

Alice felt something hit her neck, and while she would not feel pain like humans did, she knew it had been a close call. She had her rifle up at her shoulder and saw the Red Queen disappear inside a nearby building. Alice ran towards her, jumping over an overturned barrel and flattening herself against the wall as bullets tore through the plaster and bricks in front of her. Glancing around the corner she fired a burst, not expecting to hit much but at least hoping it would cause the Red Queen to take cover while Alice sought a new position.

Li dove as the glass shattered in front of her,

showering her with shards that tore into her face. Bloodied, she screamed in rage as she saw Alice run to the other side of the building, presumably to try and enter it through the side door. Li took out a grenade from her belt and threw it towards the door Alice was headed for. Alice saw the dark object land just feet in front of her and dove to her left as the grenade exploded. The wall she had dived behind took much of the impact of the explosion but she felt a tug at her leg. Looking down, everything below her knee was a mess of blood and skin. But it still moved normally, so she wasn't out of action yet.

Tso motioned for the two APCs behind him to stop. His squad had joined up with more than fifty Red Guards who had managed to fight their way into Wonderland and were now proceeding block by block. They had come across only two Biters whom they had shot with ease, but what had shocked them was the resistance they were facing from the human citizens. Tso had seen two conscripts walk up to wave to a woman in a window only to see her shoot them both before rockets fired by the other Red Guards had blown her apart. It seemed like every human in Wonderland was trying to fight them, and while many of them were clearly not trained fighters, in the congested city ruins Tso and his men were paying for every block they secured with blood. When he had asked for support, he had been told that an armored column was on its way, with more than a dozen APCs laden with Red Guards. The two APCs he saw behind him now were the only ones that had survived ambush after ambush with RPGs and grenades on the outskirts of Wonderland. He had been ordered to his current position to go to the help of a female Special Forces officer reportedly inside Wonderland, known by the code name of Red Queen.

Arjun had been stalking the group of Red Guards for some time. He knew they had inflicted heavy losses on the Red Guards, but it was impossible to seal every entry route into the sprawling ruins. Also, with attack helicopters buzzing around in the skies, the defenders of Wonderland had also paid a steep price. Satish's missile teams had inflicted heavy damage but the reality was that they had only a small stock of surface to air missiles and it was impossible for them to knock down every single helicopter when the first waves of air attacks came. In the brutal fighting that had raged for the last two hours, the helicopters had by and large disappeared, after their pilots discovered that in such congested areas, with every rooftop bristling with machine gun toting men, women and children, missiles were not the only things that could bring them down. Arjun had been in a particularly vicious firefight with a dozen Red Guards, and with years of practical training in urban warfare he had lured them into ambush after ambush, thinning their ranks until he cornered the last three and he and his men killed them in close combat. But the fighting had taken its toll on his men as well. He had started the last skirmish with three hardened fighters, all of whom were now dead, and two young boys he had using as runners and scouts. In the chaos of the last battle, he had lost track of both of them. So now it was just him, following this group of Red Guards and APCs. There was no way he could hope to cause more than nuisance value before they gunned him down, so instead of attacking he was on the radio with Danish, trying to coordinate reinforcements.

'Looking Glass, where are White Rook and his pawns?'

'No idea whatsoever. They are still mixing it up on the outskirts. I imagine White Rook has his hands full there since I haven't heard from him in more than an hour.'

Arjun grunted in frustration. He had known this would be ugly, but he had never really bargained for just how unprepared many people in Wonderland were from the months of sitting around and squabbling over domestic disputes and fawning over the toys the Central Committee had sent. Other than some of his and Satish's men, and of course Alice, most of the other adults had not even fired a gun in the last year. The comforts of city living had made them forget that freedom was a fragile gift that they could be called upon to defend at any time.

The Red Guards turned a corner up ahead and Arjun took a shortcut through two abandoned buildings, coming abreast them as they passed. Then, suddenly, the Red Guards stopped. Their officer seemed to be telling them to go slow. Arjun raised his scope to his eyes and saw what the Red Guard officer had seen.

It was Alice, locked in a hand-to-hand struggle against a girl in a Red Guard uniform inside a nearby building. The Red Queen. One of the Red Guards near Arjun raised his rifle, trying to take a shot, and Arjun knew that terrible odds or not, he could not leave Alice to be attacked from behind like this. He took his last remaining grenade and was about to pull the pin when he saw dark shapes emerge from the buildings around the Red Guards. Next he heard screams from the Red Guards as they were pulled away.

Alice's Biters had come to the rescue.

Tso had ordered his sniper to take out the Yellow Witch when his men started screaming. Biters were streaming out of the adjoining buildings and at such close quarters, his men were being massacred. He shouted for the APCs to open fire and a burst from one of their turret mounted guns mowed down several Biters, but then the Biters were too close for the APCs to fire with their heavy weapons. Tso saw a Biter with bunny ears bite into one of his men and throw the bloodied body aside. The Biter then faced Tso, looking at him with his lifeless eyes. Tso had his rifle ready, but when he saw a dozen more Biters emerge from the shadows, he knew that it would be suicide to make a stand. He shouted for his men to retreat and they clambered atop the APCs as they backed down the street, Tso firing at the hordes as they rolled away. The Red Queen would have to fend for herself for now. He radioed back and heard Commissar Hu himself at the control center. Where was General Chen? The Commissar had never seen combat and without Chen to guide them, the Red Guards were stumbling along, losing far more men than was necessary. The Commissar asked Tso to take another route, saying that the Yellow Witch had to be destroyed and also that another group of APCs was on the way.

Danish was having a hard time making sense of the mass of confused radio transmissions. He had heard the term the fog of war, but had never truly appreciated it until now. The main armored forces had been stopped but at least two groups of APCs had entered Wonderland, and from the last reports the scouts had sent in, Alice was alone and right in the middle of where both armored groups were converging.

~* * * ~

Alice felt the knife tear through her right hand, taking with it a chunk of flesh near the elbow. Li brought the knife back for another strike, but Alice blocked it, trapping Li's knife hand between the palms of both of her hands. Before Li could bring her left hand up to strike, Alice headbutted her, sending her staggering back against the wall.

After a few minutes of stalking each other through the building, Alice and Li had finally come face to face at close quarters. Both their rifles were lying on the floor by their feet, their magazines empty, and now the two adversaries were grappling hand to hand. For a minute Alice had been without her knife, losing it in the scuffle, but as Li regained her balance she snatched it back up. The two circled each other, and Alice saw that while Li's lifeless eyes betrayed no emotion, she was spitting and hissing. What had made her so angry? Li struck out again with her knife and Alice brought her left hand up, deflecting the blow, and as Li overextended, Alice turned on one foot, slamming her right elbow hard against the back of Li's head. Li crashed against a window, shattering the glass. When she faced Alice again, her face was covered with several cuts and gashes.

Alice knew that Li was a more formidable opponent than any human she could have faced. Like Alice, Li would not tire, would not feel pain, and would not stop unless Alice managed to put a knife or a bullet in her head. However, at such close quarters, Alice held the advantage. Li had been trained in the martial arts from an early age, but unlike Alice, she had not spent her youth fighting to survive every day in the Deadland.

Li snarled and lunged, bringing her knife up in an arc. Alice blocked the blow, elbowed Li in the face with her left hand and then followed through with a knife strike to the throat. Li pulled back, the knife still embedded. She felt no pain, but she wanted to scream at this witch, to tell her of all she had caused her to lose—but all she could manage was a sickening gurgle. Blood and spittle bubbled up at her mouth and she spat at Alice.

Alice turned her face away as the bloody spittle hit her and that gave Li the opening she needed. She sliced at Alice's left wrist, cutting through veins, and as blood spurted out the knife fell from Alice's grasp. Li brought her knife up, aiming at Alice's head, but Alice moved out of the way, backing up. As Li closed in, Alice pivoted on one foot and kicked, catching Li in the solar plexus. As Li staggered back, Alice rushed at her, pushing her like a battering ram straight through the window. Both of them landed on the street outside, covered in shattered and bloodied glass fragments, and as Li tried to get up, Alice smashed her head into the bridge of Li's nose, shattering it. Alice reached down and pulled her knife out of Li's neck, but before she could strike, Li managed to get her foot up and kick Alice off, and the two once again faced each other, knives in hand, circling each other.

Several bullets hit the wall around Alice and she felt at least one tear through her shoulder as she dove to the ground. A full squad of Red Guards was approaching now, guns trained on her. Li roared in frustration. She wanted to finish the Yellow Witch herself, but she was unable to speak, her vocal cords severed. So she raised her hand, signaling for the Red Guards to cease fire.

Tso ordered his men to pause. He had left the APCs behind and come through the buildings, fighting a running battle with Biters and human defenders, trying to get to the Special Forces officer he had been ordered to aid. Now he was finally close enough to look at her through his scope and he stopped in horror. She looked like a Biter. Both of them did: the Yellow Witch they had been tasked to kill and this mysterious Special Forces officer called the Red Queen. What was going on?

Alice took advantage of the momentary lull in the fighting to take cover behind a wall. There were at least a dozen fully armed Red Guards and the damn Red Queen. Armed with only a knife, Alice knew she would not last long. She tried to move to the open area to her right but a volley of fire from one of the Red Guards pinned her down.

Several of Tso's men had seen what he had and one of them asked, 'Sir, that Red Queen is a Biter. I thought our mission was to save people here from Biters.' Tso had no answer to that, but he did have a mission to accomplish. He ordered his men to fan out.

They had the Yellow Witch trapped behind the wall and he would finish her. He saw the Red Queen approaching, and he felt himself pull back at the stench and recoil at her blood-covered appearance. What was a monster like this doing in a Red Guard uniform? Li held out her hand and grabbed an assault rifle from one of the men and then she started walking towards the position where Alice was trapped.

Glass crunched underfoot as Li approached. So this is how it all had to end; surrounded, outnumbered, trapped. Alice felt no regret or sorrow. She had no real life to look forward to anyways and the way she figured it, she had already died thrice. First when she had looked on as her father and his friends were massacred at their settlement; second when she had looked upon the charred remains of her mother and sister, killed in an air strike; and finally that day when she had ceased to be Alice Gladwell and become the Queen of Wonderland. She closed her eyes, thinking back to everything she had gone through. If it all had to mean something, to be worth anything, then she could not let Wonderland be taken without one last fight. If she was going down, she would take as many of her adversaries down with her. Growing up in the Deadland, she had been taught from an early age that there was nothing worse than becoming one of the undead. Better dead than undead. That had been the motto drilled into her during combat training. But in the past few years, she had learnt that there *was* something worse than that: losing one's freedom.

Better undead than unfree. She wondered what her teachers would have said to that as she stepped out, knife in hand, ready for the inevitable.

~* * * ~

Tso heard the helicopter fly in, and looked up to

see its sleek, black shape. He grinned at his men. Finally, they were going to get reinforcements, and hopefully a helicopter ride out of this hellhole. He waved to the helicopter and as the chopper came lower, the side door slid open.

Something was wrong. The man handling the Gatling gun was not wearing a Red Guard uniform. Tso screamed at his men to take cover as the gun opened fire, spitting death at the Red Guards below. More than half of Tso's men were cut to ribbons in the first burst and as the rest tried to take cover, Biters appeared from the alleys behind them. Tso knelt and shot one in the head, but there were too many of them. Tso ordered his men to retreat into the buildings and as they ran across the street, another burst from the helicopter's gun killed two more of his men.

Alice did not know where the helicopter had come from but Li had been distracted enough by its sudden appearance to give her a window of opportunity. Alice ran towards Li as fast as she could. Growing up, that had been Alice's claim to fame: the fact that she could outrun anyone in her settlement. Li tried to bring her rifle up, but she was too late. Alice held on to the rifle with both hands and slammed it back into Li's face, the butt impacting against Li's already shattered nose and pushing broken bone fragments back into Li's brain.

The last thing Li saw was the Yellow Witch looking at her.

The helicopter landed in the middle of the road and Satish and six of his men jumped out, training RPGs at the building where the Red Guard officer and his men had taken refuge. The Biters were now streaming towards the building, and Alice took out the book from her belt, holding it above her head.

'Stop!'

The Biters stopped where they were, and Bunny Ears emerged from the crowd. Alice looked at the building and called out to the Red Guards, 'Surrender now or we will kill you.'

One of Tso's men, a conscript barely out of his teens, was crying like a baby, and the other remaining soldier looked to be in shock. Tso knew he was finished, and while he might have been tempted to try and make a last stand, he did not want to be responsible for the deaths of these two boys. There had been quite enough bloodshed today, and for a cause that he was no longer sure of. Looking at the shattered body of the Red Queen, he realized that they had been fighting a war that had been based on lies. He stepped out of the building, his hands above his head, and walked towards Alice.

'I am the officer here. If you want, take me, but let my men go.'

Studying the man's nametag for an instant, Alice said, 'Captain Tso, nobody else needs to die today. We will see you to the outskirts tomorrow, but please don't come back to Wonderland and remember to tell your masters that we are free and will fight to preserve that freedom.'

As Satish's men took Tso and his men into custody, Alice walked up to the helicopter. The cockpit window was open and she looked in to see Vince, grinning at her.

'The White Knight had to come to the rescue of the Queen today, I guess.'

~* * * ~

'Looking Glass, sector 9 is clear.'

It was now early morning, and Danish had barely slept a single minute, hearing reports as one sector after another was cleared by Satish, Arjun or their men. Much of the previous day had been consumed by fighting, street by street, house by house. The tide had finally turned when Bunny Ears and his Biters had joined the battle. Their initial arrival in the middle of Wonderland had caused many defenders to be alarmed, and indeed a few Biters had been shot down by Wonderland's panicked residents. Remarkably, however, Bunny Ears and his band had not attacked a single citizen of Wonderland, instead focusing on fighting the Red Guards and the Biters the Red Queen had brought with her. With Vince joining the defense, they had managed to get some air support, both to attack Red Guard units and also to provide advance warning of incoming units.

By five in the evening, the battle had become one of attrition, and finally Red Guard units had begun to collapse and surrender en masse. Alice had struck a goldmine by capturing a young officer named Tso. During his debriefing with Arjun and Satish, he had confessed that the rank and file of the Red Guards had no idea about the Red Queen and her Biters. He had felt betrayed and was bitter about the loss of so many of his men for a mission that had turned out to be a lie. Tso's testimony had been broadcast on the Red Guard radio frequency and while Commissar Hu was quick to call it a fabrication, Danish had no doubts that it helped convince many of the Red Guard units in the city to give up and pull back.

The night had been one of securing the borders, mopping up any last resistance, and of taking stock of the terrible losses they had suffered.

Finally, Satish, Arjun, Vince and Alice arrived at the Looking Glass. All the men were dead tired, and both Satish and Arjun had several bandages to cover wounds from shrapnel or flying glass. The most fearsome sight of all, however, was Alice. Her hands and feet were a bloody mess and she seemed to be cut in a dozen places.

'Alice, are you ok?'

Hearing the concern in Danish's voice, Alice managed a smile. 'I'm ok. Being half undead has a few advantages.'

As they sat down, Vince told them about his journey. He had reached Calcutta, and within a day a Dakota had landed as the Americans had promised. While he had sent Edwards back to America, he had decided to come back after refueling from stocks left at the old airport.

'What made you come back? You could have gone home, Vince.'

Vince looked at Satish. 'I was a United States Marine. I saw action in Iraq and Afghanistan, and we all thought that if we ever died in combat, it would at least be while serving our nation. Instead my mates were butchered by hired guns after we were betrayed by one of our own once we refused to fly for the Red Guards. I was carted off to a labor camp, where I lived the life of a slave. So I would never give up the chance to finally fly in combat again and be what I once was. Besides, the general wanted me to come back with something for you guys.'

'The general?'

'General Konrath, Alice. He's the leader of the American resistance in the Deadland there. He is one stubborn man; I'll give him that. Do you know they lost five Dakotas and their crew before they managed to get one as far as Calcutta?'

Alice wondered why anybody would go to such lengths and sacrifice so much.

'Because he knew that the only hope for lasting peace lies in humans coming to terms with Biters. Two things can make that happen: the vaccine, which hopefully Edwards is working on right now, and you. Your voice, your story could change how people in America view Biters. Many there have heard of you but they dismiss you as nothing more than a fairy tale or myth.'

'How could I possibly get to them, Vince? You know our computers have all been disabled by the Red

Guards from communicating with the Americans.'

Vince reached into his backpack and took out a large tablet.

'The general sent this. Now you can communicate all you want with the Americans.'

That afternoon, Alice walked through Wonderland. The damage and losses had been high. Despite their lack of training and practice, the people of Wonderland had fought to protect their freedom with a ferocity that even Alice had not anticipated. Whole families had perished in battle, and she had heard of small boys and girls setting off bombs that their fallen parents had laid. Despite the terrible losses, she felt a surge of hope. If there was one thing her own journey had taught her, it was the fact that liberty was secured not by a handful of heroes and champions, but when every ordinary citizen gathered up the courage to stand up against tyranny.

Bunny Ears and his Biters were waiting, so Alice approached.

'You did really well, Bunny Ears. Thank you for your help.'

Bunny Ears seemed to have lost an ear in the fighting and his face was a bloody mess, but he grunted and all the Biters knelt before Alice. Then Alice saw something that she had never seen before. People began streaming out of their houses, many still bloodied and bandaged, and they stood beside the Biters.

One of them, an old man who had served on Arun's Cabinet, spoke up, his head bowed as if not wanting to look Alice in the eye. 'Alice, please do forgive us doubting you. We are free today because of you.'

Alice raised him up.

'No. We are free today because we stood together. Let us never forget that.'

Satish had walked up behind Alice and he took in the sight before him, hundreds of humans and Biters, united in something for the first time.

'Alice, you know what you said about Biters needing symbols to follow a leader? It's not just Biters; humans need symbols to believe in as well. For the Biters, that symbol is that old book. For these people, that symbol is you.'

The rest of the day was spent beginning the monumental task of cleaning, and the Biters returned to the Reservation, though this time Alice noticed that nobody turned on the electrified fence or locked the gate.

That evening, Alice went to the Looking Glass, where Danish hooked her up via the new tablet the Americans had sent. It had a camera on it, and Alice soon found herself looking at a grizzled, bearded face.

'Alice, I am General Konrath, but you may call me Jack. Danish has been telling me about your battle, and the tale of your victory is being spread far and wide across America. Now, all we need is for you to share your story with our people. The camera will record everything you say.'

Alice spoke for the next twenty minutes, starting with her childhood, her life in the settlement at the Deadland, the day she jumped into a hole after a Biter, and then the adventure that had followed. Reliving it all left her emotionally drained, and while Biters did not cry, she knew those who heard could feel the pain that could only come from reliving the loss of loved ones.

'Thank you, Alice. One day we will meet, and our battles for freedom will become one. By the way, Danish knows of one more operation you could lead. Good night.'

Alice looked at Danish, who was grinning.

'What did he mean?'

'The Americans have managed to hack into the Central Committee's servers and broadcast systems. We can do this only once, because I'm sure the Central

Committee will block all further transmissions, so we have to make it count.'

'What do you mean?'

Danish pointed to the tablet the Americans had sent. 'Reports of the battle for Wonderland are spreading through the Mainland. Many Red Guard officers have been arrested for questioning orders, and it seems General Chen is also in custody after he refused orders to assault the city. Their plan is unraveling and once those veterans are killed or carted off to labor camps, you can bet their families and comrades will seek answers. The Mainland has been brimming with discontent, and one spark is all it will take to set it off. That spark could be you. They have made you out to be either something scared conscripts have dreamed up, or an evil witch. Seeing you, hearing you in your own voice, hearing all you have gone through, hearing about the Red Queen and her Biters, could change that. Also, Satish had recorded Captain Tso's testimony. So far only some Red Guards have heard it on their radios. Now we can broadcast it to every citizen in the Mainland. But we have only a few minutes that the Americans can assure us of. So let's get started.'

Alice held the tablet in her hands after Danish had told her they were ready. The people of Wonderland were gathered around the TVs, and they saw the usual news broadcast and soap operas replaced by Alice's face. That same face was now being streamed into millions of homes in Shanghai, Guangzhou and Beijing.

Commissar Hu was in Shanghai, dreading his meeting with the Central Committee the next morning, where he would have to explain how their plan to conquer Wonderland had turned into a bloody fiasco. He whirled around in shock as he heard the voice on TV. The most devastating salvo in this long and bloody war had been fired, not from a gun or a missile launcher, but from a small, glass covered room called the Looking Glass. That was perhaps appropriate because in any war against tyranny, the most effective weapon is not a bullet or missile but the freedom of information. Hu held his breath as Alice started speaking, her yellowed eyes looking straight at the camera.

'People of the Mainland, your Central Committee calls me a witch and a terrorist, but today I want to speak to you directly so that you may know the full truth of the war they have been waging. My name is Alice Gladwell, and this is my story.'

EPILOGUE

Two months later

ALICE AND THOUSANDS of other citizens of Wonderland were at the airport, eagerly awaiting their visitors. Danish had reported that the plane had left Calcutta over two hours ago, and it could be arriving at any time. Vince was already airborne in his helicopter to watch for any Red Guards who might pose a problem, but that possibility was remote. Red Guards were seldom seen anywhere in the Deadland, though the people of Wonderland had learnt their lesson well. That lesson was the fact that freedom from the shadow of tyranny was not one that was earned or kept easily, but required constant vigilance. So Satish and his men were, as usual, roaming the Deadland in their jeeps and captured APCs, making sure that there was no danger lurking anywhere near Wonderland. Arjun and Alice had been busy helping repair the damage to Wonderland and making sure the many hundreds of wounded and displaced got medical care and new homes. Bunny Ears and the Biters still preferred to roam in the open spaces of the Deadland but every night they returned to the Reservation, where Alice would meet them and read to them from the charred and damaged book she carried.

Of all of them, only Danish felt as if he had little work to do any more. Alice's transmission had unleashed a firestorm of dissent in the Mainland. Crowds had gathered in the streets, demanding to know the truth. Friends and relatives of imprisoned Red Guards had attacked official buildings, and most disturbingly for the Central Committee, units of Red Guards had started to rise in open mutiny. Within weeks, the Central Committee had done what tyrannies often do: shut off the flow of information in the hope that would silence dissent. All networks from the Mainland were down and the TV showed only propaganda speeches of the Commissar and old footage of Red Guard parades and exercises. That did have one side benefit for the people of Wonderland: No longer slaves to soap operas beamed through the TVs, they quickly found other, perhaps more useful ways to spend their evenings.

Alice heard Vince on the radio.

'White Queen, the White Knight sees the White King approach.'

Alice strained to see a black speck in the sky, which soon resolved into a propeller driven airplane. Danish had been in daily contact with the Americans and knew that over the last month, they had converted Calcutta into a fully operational base, with a serviceable runway and a permanent detachment of Marines to guard it against any Red Guard attacks. For now, that was not really a worry, since the Red Guards seemed to have their hands more than full with the unfolding chaos in the Mainland.

The plane landed and taxied towards the old terminal building. The thousands of people waiting burst into uproarious applause. A ladder was lowered, and a moment later Edwards descended. He smiled broadly at Alice and walked towards her, his arms outstretched.

'My girl, it can now finally be over.'

Alice had heard from Danish about how Edwards and his colleagues had used her blood samples to make a vaccine, which had already been tested on humans in America. Just the knowledge that what the Biters represented was not some supernatural evil but a disease that could be vaccinated against had proved to be a turning point in how people in America viewed Biters. Together with Alice's testimony, it had at one stroke done away with the fighting between man and Biter, and together with the turmoil in the Mainland had meant that the Red Guards had largely retreated from America as well. A cure was the next frontier, and Edwards was already working on it.

Next down was General Konrath. Alice had seen him before on video but this was the first time she had seen him in person. After they greeted each other, she and the general made a speech to the people gathered. A speech where the general reminded people that if any good had come out of the years of struggle and bloodshed, it was that people had learnt just how precious and fragile freedom could be.

That evening, the general was sitting with Alice and her friends in the Council building. He was to fly out the next morning, and the question he asked was one he had already posed twice before in the evening.

'Alice, are you sure you don't want to come along with us tomorrow morning? America was where your parents were from; that was your home.'

Alice shook his hand and smiled. 'No, thank you, General. I am already home.'

The next morning at the airport, General Konrath looked at the book at Alice's belt.

'Who would have guessed a book would have had so much power. Perhaps now we can begin to write and read books again. It would be a shame if our children forgot all that we fought for.'

'General, I've heard you were a writer before

the Rising.'

The general smiled. 'Yes, I was a novelist. They started calling me General when I led the people in my neighborhood to start fighting back against the Red Guards. Alice, I am now old and tired of all the fighting. Perhaps it's time I got back to my old calling and wrote a book. It may well be the first book written after The Rising.'

'What's your book going to be about?'

Smiling, the general said, 'I still haven't thought it all through, but I do know what I'll call it.'

'What's that?'

'*Alice in Deadland.*'

~* * * ~

Chen looked out of his one good eye to see who had come to his cell. He had already lost his right eye in the beatings that had followed his imprisonment, and his left eye was also almost closed shut due to swelling and dried blood. He could not walk very well anymore and had to be dragged out to the courtyard every morning, where he was beaten by the black clad Interior Security forces of the Central Committee. Where or how his wife was, he no longer knew. In one of his beatings, he had been told that she was also on her way to a labor camp. If that was the case, Chen prayed that she was already dead.

He heard something being dumped into his cell: a young man in the blood-covered, tattered uniform of a Red Guard officer. The man looked at Chen and recognition flashed in his eyes.

'General Chen.'

Chen spat, a glob of blood hitting the floor, before he spoke.

'I am general to nobody now, young man. I just await the day they shoot me and end it all. Perhaps they have such a long list of people to execute that my turn has not yet come.'

Despite a broken nose and jaw, the officer spoke with a hint of a smile. 'Comrade General, you are very much still the commanding officer of the Ladakh based Red Guards. For the last month, I have been leading them in guerilla warfare against the liars in the Central Committee. We've assassinated four of those bastards and killed a dozen or more Interior Security officers, but it seems my luck ran out today. We still owe loyalty to you, General, and we were all inspired by the sacrifice you made to try and save all of us.'

Chen sat up straight, warmth permeating his body, bringing back emotions he had no longer thought himself capable of.

'What is your name, officer?'

The young man sat up, facing Chen, his back to the bars of the cell.

'Comrade General, my name is Captain Tso.'

'So what news of the outside, Captain?'

'The people rage against the Central Committee. Thousands of unarmed civilians have been killed in Shanghai and Beijing, but bullets cannot silence the cry for freedom. More and more Red Guards mutiny and follow my example. It is but a matter of time before the Central Committee falls.'

Chen smiled despite the pain. 'So it has been worth it after all. I had thought I would die a broken man who died for nothing.'

Tso smiled back. 'Comrade General, you should have been with me in Wonderland. In the midst of all the bloodshed and killing, I saw something wonderful, a view of how our nation can be and will be one day. People living free, ruled by those they choose, at peace with those different from themselves.'

A guard shouted from outside the cell, 'Shut up, you traitors! The Commissar himself is coming to meet you. I think today is the day you go to hell.'

But when the two guards outside began to whisper

among themselves, Chen heard snippets of their conversation that gave away what was really happening.

'The mob's been building outside all morning. They want to free all the prisoners.'

'The Commissar has said we'll execute all of them and fly out in helicopters.'

Chen heard a few shots, which he thought meant the executions had begun. But then came the sound of assault rifles being fired on full auto. It sounded like a firefight had broken out outside the prison.

A few minutes later, the cell door opened and Commissar Hu walked in. He had lost a lot of weight and Chen noticed a pronounced limp in one leg.

'Good morning, Comrade Commissar. It seems being back in the warm fraternal embrace of the Central Committee has not agreed with you.'

Hu snarled and kicked Chen hard in the ribs.

'Shut up, you fool! Have your last laugh, for I shoot both of you traitors and put an end to your misery today!'

He called to the guards, and they entered. One of them pulled Tso to one side and the other held Chen up, holding his arms behind him. Chen looked at Tso and winked with his one good eye. For the last week, he had been carrying a razor sharp shard of glass he had picked up in the courtyard during one of his beatings. He had been trying to work up the courage to slit his own wrist and end it all. Now he knew he would get a chance to put it to another use. The man holding him was strong and young, but he was an Interior Security thug, the sum total of whose combat experience came down to beating civilian demonstrators.

As Hu took out the pistol from his holster, Chen rocked his head back, making solid contact with the guard's nose. It snapped. As the guard loosened his grip on him, Chen turned and slit the guard's throat with the shard of glass.

Fumbling with the safety, Hu leveled his gun—but too late. Chen grabbed his pudgy hand, snapping the wrist and taking the weapon from him. The guard holding Tso was reaching for his gun when Tso punched him hard in the face, sending him crashing against the bars. When he tried to get up, Chen shot him dead.

Hu was now on his knees, begging for mercy. Chen wanted to say something, to remind him of just how many lives men like him had ruined, but finally he realized that no words would do justice to the rage he felt. He kicked the blubbering Commissar down and shot him once in the head.

From outside came the heavy sounds of the Interior Security guards' boots, and the continuing sounds of the firefight raging outside the prison. Even if those outside were trying to get in and rescue the prisoners, Chen doubted they would get so far inside in time. However, he felt no fear. Indeed, he felt a sense of release wash over him as he contemplated his end. He looked at Tso and smiled as the officer saluted.

'Come, my son. Today we finally fight together one last time, but this time for something we believe in.'

As Chen took aim at the first guard to come down the corridor, he realized that Hu had been so very wrong. Tyrannies fell not when people simply began to desire freedom, but when they had already attained one very special kind of freedom. Freedom from fear.

THE END

ABOUT THE AUTHOR

MAINAK DHAR IS a cubicle dweller by day and author by night. His first 'published' work was a stapled collection of Maths solutions and poems (he figured nobody would pay for his poems alone) he sold to his classmates in Grade 7, and spent the proceeds on ice cream and comics. He was first published in a more conventional sense at the age of 18 and has since published eleven books, including the Amazon.com bestseller, *Alice in Deadland*, the science fiction bestseller *Vimana* and the post-apocalyptic thriller *Zombiestan*. Learn more about him and contact him at www.mainakdhar.com.

Made in the USA
Lexington, KY
09 May 2012